he author wishes to thank Captain Harry Thomasen and Roger
ast Oat for inspiration, encouragement, and for lives
ell-lived.

ok Design by Laurie McBarnette

er illustration Meg Kelleher

rary of Congress Cataloging-in-Publication Data

ckman, Ivy.
his is your captain speaking.

ummary: Overshadowed by his successful, athletic
r brother, Tom skips soccer practice to visit a
sing home where he develops a friendship with a
ed sea captain.
. Friendship—Fiction.   2. Old age—Fiction]
tle.
R844Th   1987   [Fic]   87-14708
0-8027-6734-6
0-8027-6735-4 (lib. bdg.)

ed in the United States of America

8 7 6 5 4 3 2 1

THIS IS YOU[R]
CAPTAIN
SPEAKIN[G]

Ivy Ruckman

For Amanda,
who will be sen[...]
to Tom's feelings[...]
All the best to[...]
and yours.
Pe[...]

Walker and Company
New York

C[...]

A[...]
fo[...]
re[...]
p[...]

A[...]
th[...]

B[...]

Co[...]

Li[...]

Ru[...]

ole[...]
nu[...]
ret[...]

I.
PZ
ISB
ISB

Pri[...]

10

For
Adelaide Couture Heylmun
Loving and Beloved Grandmother

CHAPTER
· 1 ·

Mrs. Henessey, the most "with-it" teacher in junior high, loved controversy. I think she stayed awake nights dreaming up stuff that would pit one half of our language arts class against the other.

Up to Wednesday, October 17, I managed to stay neutral during her opinion polls. That day I blew up.

"What good was that old lady to anyone?" Jim Needham was saying about a character in the story we'd just read.

I swung around in my desk and glared at my best friend. "Yeah, but what if it was *your* grandma? Could you pull the plug and let her die?"

"Yeah"—his chin came up—"if she wanted me to. I'd be doing her a favor!"

Someone hooted, and I heard Carmela say "Sick!"

"Now wait—" Mrs. Henessey jumped in, her earrings swinging. "That changes things a bit, when you add 'if she wanted me to.'"

2

"What does it change?" I cried.

"I don't think it changes anything." Carmela's cheeks had gone fire red, but she was backing me up. "It's still wrong to take someone's life."

A kid who'd been waving his hand in my face said, "How's it any different from putting an animal to sleep, tell me that?"

"Yeah, how's it different?" Jim agreed. "We think that's humane, but when it comes to people—"

A straight-A girl up front threw me a frosty look. "Doesn't everything depend on the situation?" she asked.

All of a sudden I couldn't stand that girl. What did she know about old people, or about people dying, for that matter? She always acted so cool, so *mental*. Like Henessey: *Let's discuss it, class. Get our feelings out in the open.* Carmela and I were the only ones in the room who had any feelings!

Henessey slid off the edge of her desk, looking positively gleeful to have us all stirred up. I wasn't a bit gleeful. What I wanted most right then was to take the whole class over to Sunnyside with me.

"Who's it going to be?" I'd say, challenging them to put the finger on Janice or Lucky Lucy or Roger, who had cheated death several times already.

"Roger's getting right up there," I'd point out. "Might as well give it to the old captain while he's asleep this afternoon."

By then Mrs. Henessey was walking back and forth with both hands going. "Under what circumstances"— she stabbed the air with a red fingernail—"could one justify a mercy killing? The main character in our story is all alone. No family to turn to. She's old and sick, and she tells the doctor she wants to die. Is it right for society to go against her wishes?" She stopped and faced the class. "Or is her pain . . . simply beside the point?"

I thought of my dad when she said the word *pain*. He died when I was four, so I hardly knew him, but Mom said he fought to live right up to his last breath. And he suffered plenty. He had to have morphine four times a day.

My hand shot in the air again. I didn't even know what I was going to say, but I was boiling.

"Yes, Tom, go ahead."

"What if my mom or my brother Troy decided to end it all for my dad when he had leukemia?"

The class grew suddenly quiet. Except for Jim and Carmela, the new girl who lived on my street, most of the kids in that room didn't know anything about me.

"What if they had this little conference," I plunged on sarcastically, "and Mom said, 'Today's a good day to do it. You know, he's gonna die anyway so we might as well . . .' " I stopped, swallowed. I looked at the faces looking back at me, and I didn't want to go on. *What do they care? What do they care about my dad . . . or the old people. . . .*

"I think we're going to write an opinion paper on this subject, since everyone has such strong feelings. I want them handed in Monday." She scrawled *Due Mon.* on the board. "Remember, I want opinions. So don't go looking up 'mercy killing' or 'euthanasia' or 'living will' to copy someone else's words, or I'll turn you in for plagiarism, you hear?"

4

The other kids laughed, but I tuned her out. I wasn't going to write her anything. I knew it as sure as I knew I wasn't going out for soccer, even though I'd heard the coach was after me. Might as well have two teachers on my back!

When the bell rang, I couldn't get out of there fast enough.

CHAPTER
·2·

It was exactly 3:20 when I entered the carpeted lounge at Sunnyside, the sprawling brick building where I spent a lot of time after school. Just being there made me feel better.

Fresh flowers had come in and were lined up at the nurses' station. I could hear Nell's laugh rolling out from someone's room, could hear Smitty on the intercom: "An aide to room ten NOW. Is anyone alive up there on Main?"

I swiped some ice from the cart of water pitchers, then hurried along the wide east hall, saying hi to people who were up from their naps.

I waved to Janice, who was in her wheelchair arranging yellow and orange chrysanthemums in a vase. She was singing "Oh, Danny Boy" in a high, silvery voice, but she waved back.

I spoke to Richard and Mr. Lorenzo as I cruised by. Shuffling along in plaid slacks and suspenders, they appeared to be competing with their walkers—seeing who could go slowest. *But they haven't given up yet!*

I was still smoldering over the shouting match we'd had in English that day. Sure, the Sunnyside residents were old. Some were handicapped or sick. Some were all three, but what of it? They were people. And they were my friends.

I passed spaghetti-thin Lucky Lucy, asleep, parked in the doorway of her room. Her knitting was half-on, half-off her lap. Grinning, I picked up the ball of fuzzy yarn and put it in her side carrier. She never went down for naps, afraid she'd miss something. If Jim Needham had his way, she'd be put to sleep for good.

I was part way along the sunny south hall, having fetched a drink for Nanny Henderson, when I heard Roger's voice booming out over the entire men's wing: "WILL SOMEBODY GET A NURSE IN HERE?"

If anyone was still trying for some afternoon shuteye, forget it.

"I WANT SOME TOILET PAPER—AND I WANT IT NOW!"

I took off running, practically hurtling myself around the corner onto West. Halfway up the hall I saw Natalie in her pink uniform running toward me.

"Here," she said, pushing a roll of paper into my stomach, "take this in to him."

The sight of Natalie cheered me no end. She was the youngest aide at Sunnyside—the friendliest, too.

"NUUUUUUUURSE!" bellowed Roger again. "I'M WARNING YOU!"

I tore into room eighteen and handed the toilet paper in through the bathroom door.

"Hey, Roger . . . it's me, Tom. Are you all right?"

He calmed down a little but was still growling when he asked, "What are you doing here? You playing hooky?"

"No, it's after three, school's out. Guess what, Roger?" I raised my voice so he could hear me. "The new kit came, and you were right. It's got those cheap plastic eyebolts in it. Want to see all the stuff?"

"Of course I do." I heard the toilet flush.

I had to check in with my mother, who had been the head cook at Sunnyside for years, so I told him I'd be right back.

"Well, don't take all day," he hollered through the door. "I'll wait for you in the hold."

I went on to Mom's huge stainless-steel kitchen, where I found her mixing a chicken salad for dinner. She gave me a cushiony hug with the arm that wasn't involved in the stirring. "Have any homework?" she asked.

"Nope."

"Look at me, Tom. Not even math?"

"I did it in class, honest."

"Nice try, punk," the guy at the sink said. "I used to tell my mother the same thing."

I made a face at his back.

"I see you got your model," Mom said. "Anything else in the mail? A letter from Troy?"

"Nope. Just this and the gas bill. Oh yeah—and an ad for fur coats."

"Fur coats!" she hooted. "Oh, Tom, that'll be the day."

I knew Roger was as excited as I was to see the *Cutty Sark* all laid out. He thought a clipper ship would be a good challenge for me, and I sure as heck wanted to get my mind off school, so I hurried back to the hold.

Once a staff room, "the hold"—as we named it—was a junk room we'd taken over for our own purposes. It was full of boxes and busted-up chrome commodes and chairs Roger called "amputees" because of their missing legs. It was a great place to hang out.

A couple hours later, Roger and I were still there with pages of instructions and loose parts scattered from one end of our long table to the other. He was as excited to see the *Cutty Sark* as I was, but when he started insulting the model manufacturers, I knew he was getting tired.

"How about some grub?" I asked, hauling two packs of crackers out of my pocket—emergency food I'd smuggled from the kitchen.

"Good idea, Buddy." He ran a hand over his head, smoothing down the imaginary hairs, and leaned back in his captain's chair. He was still in an insulting mood, but he gave me one of his kindly looks anyway.

"Whoever puts out these boat kits has a head full of mush, you know that?"

I laughed.

"You listen to an old man, now. You seat that mast the way they tell you to, and your whole investment goes in the drink."

"If you say so."

"Well, I say so."

We were both laughing as I ripped the cellophane off the crackers.

I liked the way Roger's stiff gray mustache always started twitching when he got tickled about something. I also liked the way his eyes shot sparks into his glasses when he was being ornery. Some faces just sit there like an ornament on the shoulders, if you know what I mean. Not Roger's. His face was always busy, always interesting to look at.

I stuck half the crackers in Roger's right hand, which didn't shake as much as the left, then pulled my chair around so we could face each other and talk.

Roger attacked a soda cracker. Motioning off all of a sudden, he sent crumbs flying everywhere. "Why, you and I could take off in an old-timey vessel like that, if it was built right, be halfway around the world in three months."

"You think so?"

"Oh, hell yes, Buddy. With a twenty-man crew? Shoot! I'd do the navigating, you could start out as cabin boy, move up to mate. Wouldn't be long you'd be reading the sextant, smart as you are."

We talked like that all the time. One day we'd be headed for Singapore, the next we'd trade fish for a load of salt in Spain. Rum, tea, coal—we hauled more stuff than you could think of. I never got tired of the trips we took in the hold.

"Of course," Roger said, looking off, "now that you've got a woman, you won't have any use for an old sea urchin like me. The ladies have a way of keeping a man home."

I sat up straight, pretending to be insulted. "Woman! First *I* heard about it."

"Oh, you know . . . that . . . Carmelita. Whatever you call her. That new girl at school. Isn't she your girlfriend?"

"Carmela? She's not my girlfriend." I used to gag on the word "girlfriend," but I found myself thinking, "Not yet."

"Well, maybe she is, and maybe she isn't. I figure you won't be sailing off with Captain Ericksen much longer. A man grows up, takes on responsibilities. It's the way of the world."

"Roger," I croaked, "I'm still in junior high."

"Oh now, come on. You're sixteen or my name ain't Picklepuss."

I choked on that one.

"Yessir," he went on, "you can stow away when you're sixteen. You know that, don't you? You have to be at least sixteen."

"I never heard of such a law."

"It's Ericksen's Law," he said with a chuckle.

He swiped at the crumbs, then lifted one knee with his hands and placed it over the other. When he took out the pipe, which he rarely smoked, and put it between his teeth, I knew we were through working for the day.

"I had a stowaway on board one time, Buddy."

"You did?"

"Strangest thing . . . We'd set out from St. Johns one gray morning with a load of fresh cod. A fifteen-year-old flyweight, hardly bigger'n you, sneaked onto that tern schooner while we were loading her, unbeknownst to the whole lot of us."

"Where'd he hide? What happened?"

"A killer storm's what happened. Before nightfall we

were beset by hurricane-force winds. Seas so heavy . . . we had every man on deck and wished for more—"

"THOMAS J. PALMER!" came Mom's voice, making me jump. "Do you have Roger in there?"

She couldn't see us around the boxes, but the light gave us away.

"Yeah, we're right here," I answered.

"Dinner was served thirty minutes ago. What are you thinking of? Get Roger to the dining room or you're both in big trouble, you hear me?" The door shut with a bang.

I waited as Roger pocketed his pipe, then I handed him his cane and turned off the light. "It's okay," I said, noticing his guilty look. "Mom never stays mad for long."

By the time we got there, people were finished and leaving. The big dining room, with its glass chandeliers, bluebird wallpaper, and row of sunny windows, was practically empty.

Brooke was putting dirty trays into their slots on the rack. Cody Stoddard, another teenage volunteer, was moving wheelchair people into the hall.

Lucky Lucy put on her brakes long enough for Roger to pat her on the shoulder, and they smiled at each other. "See you at Bingo tomorrow," he said. He claimed her good fortune rubbed off on other people, and *that's* why he sat by her at Bingo.

By the time the two of us got trays, he'd either forgotten the story he was telling, or he was too hungry to talk. Roger ate his chicken salad and roll without once looking up.

I waited until he finished dessert. Finally, I had to ask, "What happened to that stowaway?"

He looked up, wiped his mouth with a napkin. "Lowell Max was his name. Became my chief mate a dozen years later. As good a man as ever went to sea."

"Did you turn him in? Did he get arrested?"

"A German submarine got him. He was crossing the Atlantic on the *Lucy Deever* . . . part of a convoy. She was well ballasted on that trip, could stand up to the worst kind of gale. It's contrary to nature"—he thrust out his hand and wriggled it like a fish—"sneaking around *under* a ship!"

He'd jumped ahead on the story and was remembering Lowell Max long after he was sixteen. When Roger's chin began to quiver, I looked down and concentrated on my butterscotch pudding.

Pretty soon, I heard him fumbling for his pipe, heard him clamp down on the stem.

"I wish I could take you on an ocean voyage with me, Buddy. Rolling and tumbling in those great waves"—the pipe clicked as he talked—"it's something a man never forgets."

I could tell he wasn't putting me on the way he did about half the time, but we both knew we'd never go to sea together. Roger was eighty-seven years old, for crying out loud, and I was just a kid. Besides, Sunnyside was a thousand miles inland. The only ships around there were the models we built in the hold.

I gave him back a steady gaze all the same. "I'd go with you, too," I said. And I meant it.

CHAPTER
·3·

Naturally, I didn't tell Carmela in the note that I was taking her to Sunnyside after school. I wasn't sure she'd go if she knew.

When the last bell rang, I slipped through the north door of John Glenn Junior High so the soccer coach wouldn't see me, then hung around in front of the dry cleaners a few minutes. Carmela was alone when I finally spotted her coming toward me on the sidewalk.

"Hey, Tom!" She waved and broke into a run, her black hair bouncing on her shoulders.

I looked away so she couldn't see my silly grin, thinking how much I like girls who act natural. Phonies I can't stand, the stuck-up snobs who are just too prissy to live.

Carmela's more like my friend at Sunnyside who works the three-to-eleven shift. I made a list one day, thinking how I'd describe Natalie if I were doing a profile for *People* magazine. I put down words like clean, home grown, fresh, unspoiled. "Sounds like an ad for broccoli," Mom said when she found the list on my dresser. Anyway, Carmela's that kind of girl, too, only she's my age. Natalie's nineteen. "And aging fast," she tells everyone.

"I found the note you stuffed in my locker," Carmela said when she caught up with me. "Where we going?"

"It's a surprise. Sure your mom won't care?"

"She's at work, but I'll have to call her." She flashed me one of her perfect smiles and my palms turned sweaty. Suddenly, I began to have second thoughts about what I was doing. What made me think Carmela would like going to Sunnyside, anyway?

But she made with a little skip that let me know she was happy. "Mr. Thurston is going to be so mad at you, missing soccer again. How come you signed up?"

"I didn't. Mom did. Now she doesn't want to suit up either."

Carmela laughed. "I looked for you yesterday, but you took off like a roadrunner. I'll bet you went to McDonald's for one of those free drinks they're advertising."

"Nope."

"Where do you go after school every day?"

"Aw, you don't want to know," I teased.

She pressed her lips together and gave me a disgusted look. "Would I ask if I didn't want to know, hmmmmmmm?"

Seeing her dark eyes in full sparkle, I decided I liked having her be curious about me. If 1) you're slightly pudgy and 2) your brother wins distinction in sports without even trying and 3) it's your mother who signs you up for soccer (a game for people with one left foot, one right foot), you'd better get a little mystery going about yourself if you want to impress a girl.

Carmela was polite enough not to ask any more questions, so I quickly changed the subject back to school. Soon we were laughing about how her applesauce slipped off her lunch tray at noon and splashed the vice principal's socks.

"I wanted to die when everyone clapped!" she said shyly.

Listening as she chattered on about school, I sneaked another look at her rosy cheeks and creamy skin. I thought again how perfect her name was for her. I fell in love with her name the first day of school, when she was still the new girl answering roll call with a politeness and accent I wasn't used to.

Later, when we discovered we lived on the same block, we ended up walking to school together most days. She didn't have a best friend yet; I'd lost mine. When Jim Needham became our soccer team's one-and-only hope, he and I sort of split up for the season. (After yelling at each other in English class, we had probably split up for good.)

Too soon we were turning the corner onto Parkway. The word SUNNYSIDE—in bright yellow letters—hit me right in the eye. A big, stiff sunflower decorated the redwood sign, and the words "A Convalescent and Nursing Facility" were written across the bottom of it.

I was still sweating, I guess, because the breeze coming through my T-shirt felt good.

I wished Carmela would keep on talking, but suddenly she seemed to notice where we were going, too.

"We turn in here," I said.

She gave me a funny look. "Oh, is this the surprise?"

I grinned, but didn't answer. We headed up the sidewalk, past the crazy-quilt beds of flowers: marigolds, mums, blazing red salvias. She was impressed that I knew their names.

Sunnyside, looking like an oversized ranch-style house, sits back off the street with a circle drive in front and another that goes all the way around the building. A pick-up/delivery roof juts out to cover the entry. Joe Hickson, the maintenance man, was up on a ladder that day, rehanging the LOW CLEARANCE sign that people were forever knocking down with their campers.

"Not again!" I exclaimed, wanting to delay going inside with a little conversation.

"Everybody keeps tryin' to raise the roof!" he said between hammer blows.

As soon as we got inside, Carmela's nose started twitching.

"That's the stuff they put in the scrub buckets," I hurried to explain.

"Disinfectant? It doesn't smell like disinfectant."

I was used to the smell, myself. "Let's go to the kitchen. My mom works here. She said she'd be baking pineapple-upside-down cake today and she'll give us a piece."

Walking along the main hall, I explained to Carmela that Sunnyside was *home* to all kinds of people who couldn't take care of themselves.

"Really? It kind of looks like a hospital."

"You'd think it was if you didn't know better, but people have their own chairs and pictures and TVs and stuff."

"So they just . . . *live* here?"

"Yeah. It's a nursing home. In volunteer training, they tell us to call people residents, not patients." I broke out laughing. "Of course, Roger, this guy I know, claims he's a prisoner. But that's only when he's mad."

At the nurses' station we ran into Natalie in her pink aide's uniform, dearranging two baskets of flowers. My face got hot when I realized I'd have to make introductions, but she spoke up and saved me.

"Oh boy, am I glad to see you!" Quickly she added, "Both of you. Can you do me a favor, Buddy? Janice is waiting in the activity room. Would you mind carrying these down to her so she can get them ready for the dinner tables? Wait—I'll get some vases—"

Natalie, not to be confused with the White Tornado, was in and out of the supply room in a flash. She loaded Carmela's arms with flowers, mine with vases and baskets. Acting fast so Smitty, the supervisor, wouldn't catch her, she pulled off a length of butcher paper, rolled it up, tucked it under my chin. "Thanks, Buddy, I'm an hour behind and I just got here."

Then she bent down to Carmela's level. "I'm Natalie. What's your name?"

"Carmela Rice."

"I'm very happy to meet you," Natalie said, friendly as anything.

I took off for the activity room with Carmela trailing behind. I wanted to explain that Janice had been an interior decorator during her working days and was bored out of her skull at Sunnyside until Natalie started having her do flower arrangements. When flowers are donated from funerals and weddings, Natalie dearranges (that's what I call it) those nice bouquets to give Janice a chance to make them up again.

Carrying the roll of paper under my chin, I couldn't explain anything.

"Hello, Janice," I said when we got there. The sun streaming in behind her wheelchair made a fuzzy halo of her white hair and fringed her blue sweater with gauze.

"Buddy, dear, how nice to see you. And who's this?"

"She's a friend from my school." I spread the butcher paper on the table and laid out the flowers. "Her name's Carmela."

"How lovely! I'm charmed." Janice put out her hand. "I've heard such nice things about you."

I poked Carmela with my elbow so she'd go ahead and shake hands, which she did.

"Well, dears, could you have lunch with me at the club?" Janice asked, her bracelets jangling as she patted Carmela's hand.

"She has to phone her mom," I answered, "but next time we will. Huh, Carmela?"

I edged toward the door, but Carmela seemed fascinated enough to stay right there talking. "We better go," I reminded her.

A polite minute later we were on our way to the phone. "Did she really want to take me to her club?" Carmela asked.

"She'd take us both if she could, but Janice is out in the paw-paw patch about half the time."

"Is she . . . you mean she's . . ."

I knew she was fishing for a nicer word than "crazy."

"She gets mixed up. A lot of the old people who live here get mixed up."

Carmela made a shivery motion with her shoulders. "Doesn't it give you the creeps?"

I shook my head no.

While she called her mom, I walked away and tried to remember how it was my first day at Sunnyside. I was ten then. With Troy at football practice all the time, Mom wanted me around so she could keep her eye on me. I hated it at first. Everything was strange, and I was scared. Finally, when the staff started giving me jobs to do, I got to like it more. When Mrs. Purdy told me I could be a regular volunteer, one of a handful of kids who hung around to help after school, I thought I was pretty hot stuff.

Then Roger came. When he got interested in my models and I got interested in his real-life adventures—well!—that was when Sunnyside got to be more "home" than home sometimes.

I helped myself to a drink at the water cooler, wondering what was taking Carmela so long. I hoped she could stay.

Waiting there, nervous as anything, I mentally made the trip to the kitchen, trying to decide which residents to avoid so Carmela wouldn't get a severe case of the willies.

When she came smiling to meet me, I knew everything was okay.

"All right!" I said as we took off. "I want you to meet Roger first."

I hurried Carmela down Main toward West, though she lagged slightly behind me, trying to see into rooms as we passed.

At the corner we came face to face with Laura-the-

Kisser. Looking like the ultimate sportswoman in her burgundy sweats, she was doing a daring five knots an hour in her walker.

"Buddy!" She reached out a hand and snagged me. "Where have you been?"

"School, where else? What have you been up to, Laura?"

"Oh, going round and round! What do I ever do? Musta walked a hundred miles today." She pulled me in for a kiss on the ear and a few pats. We laughed and hugged. "See you later," I said, once she returned my hand.

We moved on, but Carmela looked back over her shoulder. "How can you let her kiss you like that? She's so old!"

"I don't know." I thought about it, shrugged. "She's got to kiss somebody. . . . I'm handy, so she kisses me."

I pushed aside a laundry rack, wondering if I'd have to explain Roger to her, too.

"Seems funny to hear everyone calling you Buddy."

"They can't remember 'Tom.' "

She giggled.

"Sometimes they can't remember 'Buddy,' either. I've been coming here for three years now, but even I can't remember who started calling me that. One lady calls me 'Sonny.' " I didn't tell her the rest—Sonny of Sunnyside Farm. (How embarrassing can you get?)

Roger was still asleep when we got to room eighteen. His was a private room, west-facing, with sun filtering in through the leaves of a red sumac. The room was so peaceful, and the hump that was Roger lay so still I wondered if we should go in.

I decided we should. I put a finger to my lips and motioned for Carmela to come along. I wanted her to see the ship's wheel Roger's daughter had had mounted for him right under the window. Three feet top to bottom, with six-inch knobs sticking out all around, it was the very wheel he'd used his last few years at sea, hauling fish up and down the East Coast. "Coasting," as he called it.

"It's from the *Mary Demoor*," I whispered to Carmela. "She's in dry dock now, but Roger was her last skipper."

I stood behind the wheel, my feet spread apart for balance, and showed Carmela how I cut a swath through the ocean. We grinned at each other. Then I moved away so she could try it. The wheel was a big, heavy thing. Beautiful, too, the mahogany worn smooth as glass, the brass joinings polished and shiny. It was magic, the way you could feel a boat moving under your feet when you touched that wheel.

Carmela looked out of the window while she steered, as if she, too, were seeing waves rising and falling.

Then I showed her the ship's lantern that hung near the door of the bathroom and whispered that it came off a fishing trawler.

I checked to make sure Roger was still breathing. His mouth was open as usual, but he wasn't snoring. For someone with such a booming voice, he sure was a quiet sleeper.

"Roger's my best friend here at Sunnyside," I said as we went on to the kitchen. "He's a retired sea captain from Grand Bank, Newfoundland. Been everywhere, ports all over the world. You should hear him talk."

"Oh, really?"

"Yeah. He's helping me do a model of the *Cutty Sark*."

"No kidding! I never saw a model of a shark before."

"*SARK!*" I had to laugh at Carmela. "*Cutty Sark*. The real one's over a hundred years old. She was the fastest clipper ship in the China tea trade. Hey, you want to go to the hold and see a picture of it?"

She shook her head. "I better not stay too long. I've got a ton of math tonight."

My heart sank. I'm no dummy.

By the time we reached the kitchen, Mom was in her big white apron, cooking dinner. She waggled her finger at me when I told her about Laura. "You're a regular kiss-and-tell, Thomas Palmer! Don't you know that isn't nice?"

Then she had us sit at a small table near the back door. She brought us each a piece of cake and a glass of milk. "Can you entertain yourselves now? I've got sixty-eight mouths to feed before long."

"Yes, thank you, Mrs. Palmer," Carmela said politely, but under her nice words I caught her disappointment.

I was disappointed, too, because Roger was to be the best part of the surprise. Sitting there staring at the top of her head, I couldn't think of a thing to say that would make her feel better. Or me, either.

I shouldn't have brought her. What was I thinking of?

After a few bites I said, "Too bad Roger's asleep. He's a neat old guy. Think you could wait around awhile?"

"I better not, honest." I got a quick smile before she went on eating cake.

I popped a section of warm pineapple in my mouth,

feeling worse by the spoonful. Finally I said, "Sunny-side's a pretty nice place, though, don't you think?"

"Hmmmmm, it's okay. I mean, it's different. Kind of depressing, you know? I guess a person would have to get used to it." She looked up. "Is this where you go every day after school?"

"No, not every *single* day."

She shrugged, took a sip of milk, grinned. "I'd go to soccer practice, I guess, if it was up to me."

CHAPTER ·4·

Six people read their papers in class on Monday. It was a sweaty time for me, but I still wasn't convinced that anyone had the right to hurry things along. Though Kim Phillips wrote an excellent paper on the living will (according to Henessey, who must have known she looked it up), I'd never sign one. Not me! I wanted to live every second of my life—right up to age one hundred, if it came to that. Roger did, too.

When Mrs. Henessey gave us our next assignment, which was to write funny epitaphs for ourselves, I thought, what *is* this? Do I have a ghoul for an English teacher?

I whipped out a sheet of paper and did mine in thirty seconds. I drew a big tombstone surrounded by scraggly grass and printed my epitaph on it:

HERE LIES TOM
WHO DIED STUBBORN

I found Roger's room empty that day after school. The floor was freshly scrubbed, the bed smooth. The flowers sitting on his TV looked like one of the rare funeral arrangements Natalie and Janice left intact.

When I checked the activity calendar on the back of his door, I saw that Monday afternoon was blank. No programs, not even a sing-along. I hated it when Roger wasn't where he was supposed to be.

I walked along the west wing, hoping to see Natalie or Smitty or someone I could ask. I glanced into Donald and Scotty's room, where Roger visited, but he wasn't there. I was halfway to the door of Jacob Salter's room when I heard "Hold still, you old coot!" I smiled with relief.

"What's the matter with you?" Roger's voice boomed. "You can't go out like that—you'll scare the ladies to death."

I got there in time to see old Jacob pounding the floor with his walker, which meant he was mad, too. I wasn't sure what was going on, but it looked as if Roger was trying to zip up Jacob's pants. Jacob, still a political activist at age ninety-eight, was acting about as friendly as a porcupine.

"Ho! No more insults!" Jacob shouted. "Go get Martin."

Roger straightened up. "Look, you called me in here. If you'd quit prancing around—"

I wanted to laugh in the worst way, hearing them carp at each other.

Suddenly Jacob spotted me. "What do you want?"

Roger swung around in slow motion.

"Buddy, say something to this old radical. He's got up another petition to be signed. Thinks he can just hobble right up to the ladies with a . . . with a gaping hole in his pants."

"Pea-brained sailor!" Jacob muttered. Then, gasping for air, "Where's th' dang nurse when you need 'im?"

"You don't need a nurse. Hold still! I can get it, I tell you." Roger moved in again.

"Don't touch me!" Jacob screamed, lunging away.

I grabbed Jacob just in time to keep him from toppling over. "Hold it, you guys. Just cool it, okay?"

Roger dropped into a chair next to the bed. "Don't ask me to sign your old paper."

"Sure, blow up the whole world, why don't you? *Nuclear nutsssss!*"

Roger threw his hands up in disgust, though I was the one getting sprayed with *s*'s.

Bending down for an inspection, I could see that particular zipper wasn't going anywhere—up or down. It was jammed good, and teeth were missing like crazy. I remembered that half Jacob's clothes come from the lost-and-found. That pair of pants should have stayed lost.

Luckily, my mom, who heard us clear over in the kitchen, came in and saved us. Right away she dug a big safety pin out of Jacob's nightstand. It didn't faze her a bit to gather up the material of his polyester slacks and pin everything shut on the outside. She straightened his shirt collar, too, when she was through. "Where's your petition, Mr. Salter?" she said. "I want to sign this one myself."

Once Roger and I were out in the hall again, I broke out laughing. I just couldn't help it.

"You knew that old rascal got called to jury duty last

week," he said, the sparks still shooting out of his eyes. "He heard they'd pay him for his time, so he was bound and determined to go to the courthouse. Took a cab, spent all that money . . . then got disqualified."

"What does that mean?"

Roger's voice turned gravelly. "When a man gets to where he can't zip up his pants, everyone figures he's too senile for jury duty. Think of it. Someone like Jacob, mind as quick as it ever was. They sent him back to Sunnyside with his tail between his legs."

"Is that what the petition is about?" I asked.

"No, no, the petition is anti-nuke something or other."

I tried to read his face. "And you're not going to sign it?"

"I've seen two world wars, Buddy, and a heap of senseless dying. You know blamed well I'll sign it." He chuckled a little. "But not today."

When his mustache turned puckery I knew he was over being mad. "Pea-brained sailor! You hear him call me that?"

I shook my head and we laughed again.

A minute later we were in Roger's room, and he was pulling a plaid scarf out of the closet.

"Let's go to the greenhouse," he said. "The *Cutty Sark* can wait. I need a walk."

I'd have rather worked on the *Sark*, of course, but what the heck? We had all winter.

Roger fished around in a drawer, then shoved a black tobacco pouch in his pocket along with his pipe. I caught his grin. What he really needed after the session with old Jacob was a smoke. With a history of heart trouble, he couldn't let the nurses catch him smoking, so every once in a while he'd sneak off. Lucky for him, the greenhouse was right next door.

Roger got his cane going, and we headed out through the lobby and across the asphalt parking lot. Leaves swirled around our feet as we walked. For an old geezer, as Roger called himself, he moved along at a pretty good clip.

"This is the season for bulbs," he reminded me, the trouble with Jacob forgotten. "You and your mom going to plant any?"

"I doubt it. She never wants to spend the money."

"Maybe I'll buy you some bulbs. Would you stick them in the ground if I did?"

"Sure I would."

Before Roger came to Sunnyside, I hardly knew a petunia from a dandelion. Now I not only recognize plants, I know some of their Latin names and a whole lot about their "personalities," as Roger would put it. He was a good teacher. Tough, too. I got poked on the shoulder with his old pipe more than once when I didn't know something he thought I should.

To tell the truth, I endured those first greenhouse lessons mostly for the soft ice cream that came afterward. If I did good, Roger would buy me a treat at the convenience store down the block. Then something changed. I developed a real thing about plants. I even started talking to my Boston fern after hearing Roger fuss over his.

"Feeling pale today, Myrtle?" he'd say to this big old lacy fern, so healthy it covered his dresser top. Then out would come the plant food, and fat Myrtle would shiver with joy. (His Myrtle and my Sam are twins. We bought them for each other last Christmas.)

In the greenhouse Roger headed straight for the bulb bins, where he began lifting and sniffing bulbs. "Better get a dozen," he told me. "Study the chart first. If you stagger the botanicals with the Breeders and Darwins, you'll get blooms all spring."

I picked out two medium-size species bulbs, held them up.

"Too small. You want a big flower, you start with a big bulb."

I put them back and started over. By the time I'd decided on all twelve, Roger had his pipe going and was sitting on a nearby stump, puffing his heart out. I never saw him happier than when he was at the greenhouse. All those years at sea, he said, made him a plant lover of the first order. A pipe lover, too, I decided, watching him suck in the smoke and blow it out into sweet-smelling layers of Cherry Blend.

I took my time at the bins, knowing this was the best part of his day.

We fooled around another twenty minutes. Roger had to poke his fingers into a few flats and pots to see if the guys who work there were doing their jobs. He once gave an employee a regular tongue-lashing when he found an Austrian pine that needed watering.

"Time for tulips again?" the lady at the cash register asked. "Those early Emperors will knock your eyes out come spring."

At the convenience store down the block we went through the same old business of me trying to pay and Roger insisting the treat was on him.

"Give him an extra dollop on that cone," Roger told the girl at the machine. Then to me, "What will it hurt? You want something else while we're here? Gum? Candy bar?" I shook my head no, but he bought some gum anyway and stuck it in my rear pocket.

"How's that girlfriend of yours?" Roger asked as we headed back.

"You mean Carmela?" I ran my tongue around the cone to catch the drips.

"That's the one. I thought you were going to bring her over. She may not be good enough for you, Buddy. Better get a second opinion."

"She came already. You were asleep."

"No!"

"Yeah, you were."

"Well, bring her again. I get tired of looking at old Jacob and Donald."

I giggled a little, thinking of the contrast. "Heck, you see Natalie every day," I reminded him.

"Don't see much of her. That girl's just a pink blur goin' down the hall."

We laughed, picturing Natalie at top speed.

"I don't think Carmela liked Sunnyside much," I told Roger finally.

"Is that right?"

"She said it was depressing."

"Hmmmmm."

"Do you think Sunnyside's depressing? I don't."

He knocked a paper cup off the sidewalk with his cane. "You're used to all of us has-beens. I reckon she's not."

"Shoot, you're not a has-been! You know more than all my teachers put together."

"We have to face it, Buddy. My future's about used up. You and Carmela, now, you've got your whole lives. Better ask her again, but be patient."

I told him I might, but I didn't make any promises.

When Roger started slowing down, I figured the trip had worn him out. He'd take a quick nap now before dinner, and I'd go on home to wait for Mom. She promised we'd go to the Pizza Hut to celebrate Troy's latest string of touchdowns.

Halfway across the parking lot, Roger stopped to knock out his pipe. He rapped it three or four times against the handle of his cane, letting ashes fly everywhere, then pocketed it before we got to the double front doors. We grinned at each other like a couple of conspirators.

"The days would get mighty long if I didn't have my old buddy," he said, mussing my hair as we went back inside.

I ducked away. "How come you call me 'the pest' if you like me so much?"

"Don't know why I do that. You figure I have a mean streak?"

Smitty, the nursing supervisor, who could sniff out a pipe at fifty yards if it wasn't stone cold, gave us a very suspicious look as we walked by with our innocent faces.

CHAPTER
·5·

Nearly a week later I was still avoiding Carmela. That made three people I was trying to avoid: 1) Carmela, 2) Mrs. Henessey, who had been giving me extra attention for some reason, and 3) Mr. Thurston, the soccer coach.

The last bell was ringing as I tore out of the north door on a dead run for home. Five more months of avoiding people, and I'd for sure be in shape for spring track. Mom would just love having another athlete in the family.

"Yeah, but there are kids who have more talent in their hands than in their feet," I told her all the time. I'd point out my soap carvings, my one-and-only painting that could be anything, depending on your mood, and, of course, the six model boats that hung on dental floss from my ceiling.

"You need to get outside," she'd say, totally unimpressed. "Run and play and have a good time while you're young. Look at Troy."

No way! All looking at Troy does is reinforce my inferiority complex.

I started thinking about food as soon as I reached the front porch. Remembering my promise to lighten up on the calories, I made myself stop to check the mail before going in. I could put off eating all the way to dinner if I had a new crafts catalog.

Unfortunately, Jim Needham saw me from across the street just then.

"Tom, you piker," he yelled, "how come you're not at practice?"

"How come *you're* not?" I yelled back.

"Forgot my shoes. Thurston says he's gonna crucify you."

"Yeah, well"—I racked my brain—"tell him I have a job."

"Ha!" He slammed into his house and disappeared.

I did have a job, but I was taking the day off. Even I got tired of Sunnyside and needed a break now and then.

The catalog I ordered still hadn't come, but I saw familiar handwriting on one of the envelopes. I checked the return address:

> *Troy Palmer*
> *Bronc Hall, Room 22 . . .*

I grinned. He wrote at last! Mom would be so tickled to have a real letter. He'd been gone six weeks, and all we'd had were two postcards telling us how hard college football was compared to high school.

"See what happens when you get to be a big-shot collegian?" Mom had said Sunday when he didn't call.

I figured it was just Troy's way. He's a fireball. He gets busy with things. "He's your dad all over again" was the way Mom put it. (What she meant, but didn't say because of my feelings, was that Troy's "athletic.")

I made myself a glass of chocolate milk, then settled down in the back-yard glider to read the letter.

I got as far as the third paragraph before seeing my name.

"Did you get Tom signed up for soccer?" he wrote. I made a face. "It's not good for him to be following you around that nursing home all the time." *Following you around!* What a crock! How would he know? I tossed the first page on the grass and read on. "In a year or so he won't want that extra weight, either, he'll want muscle. I'd like to have him here at college with me. . . ."

I stuffed the letter in the envelope when I finished. Why was he always hassling me? We were *different.* I knew it even if he didn't.

I flashed on how we used to play "Dad and Troy" when we were little, and how he almost lost his mind trying to teach me to catch a football.

"I'll be Dad, you can be me," he'd say in this cheerful voice, trying to suck me into stuff I didn't want to do. "Come on, let's go. Dad knew a ton of tricks. I'll teach you everything he taught me!"

It was easy for him to play Dad. The trouble was, no matter how hard I tried, I was never good at being Troy.

I leaned back, draining the last of the chocolate milk. While my brother was seeing himself as a football great, I was pretending to be a shipbuilder. I finally decided there must be a craftsman hidden somewhere among our ancestors, even though Mom said the Palmer men had been athletes and salesmen for three generations.

It might have helped if I could actually remember my dad. I'd never say so to Mom, but I felt more related to Roger Ericksen at Sunnyside than I did to my own father. Of course, Roger and I spent the whole summer working on my *Swan 51* sailing yacht. You get pretty chummy when you're slicing up the old balsa together.

I stretched out on the glider and watched leaves drift to the ground from our maple tree, amazed at how short my fact list on Dad really was. I knew he sold office supplies: we still had more ballpoints around the house than the three of us could use in a lifetime.

I guess he was a big jock in high school before that. However, I'd found only one picture of him in the year-book wearing a football uniform. In the other three pictures he was 1) going to a dance, 2) leaning on a table in chemistry lab, and 3) posing with the cheerleaders. I didn't know how big of a jock that made my father, James Thomas Palmer. I used to wonder if Troy made things up—or just made the stories better.

What I knew for a fact was that cancer got my dad when he was thirty-seven and I was four. Mom says he died like a real hero, fighting leukemia the same way he played football. I used to like having them tell me what a hero Dad was facing death, but as we got older, Troy didn't want to talk about it as much.

"It's like an inside sore," he told me finally. "Something you can't get to with Ben Gay . . . or anything else. So don't keep asking me, all right?"

I took my glass in to the sink and tossed the letter on the kitchen table. I was supposed to have the back yard raked when Mom got home from Sunnyside. She'd left me a note a hundred items long of things I should do if I didn't want to be thrown out on the street homeless.

I got my radio and the rake. I could stand anything if I was listening to music—even yardwork.

I was really getting in the mood, swinging my butt around to The Jingoes and imagining the rake was Carmela, when the phone rang. I hesitated. What if it was the coach? He told Jim Needham he was going to call me if I didn't show up.

It was Natalie. "I've got an emergency on my hands," she said.

I caught my breath. "Roger?"

"Oh, heavens no! It's my bike. I'm over here with a flat tire, of all things."

"You're at Sunnyside?"

"Where else?"

"I thought this was your day off." (I usually took my day off on Natalie's day off.)

"It was. It *is*, but someone gave me these cherry tomatoes, way too many to eat, so I brought some over here. Now I'm stuck with no way to get back to the apartment. You don't have a patch kit, do you?"

Does a dog have fleas?

"Meet me in back," I said. "I'll be there in five."

I threw "Carmela" on the leaf pile, tore into the garage for my tool kit, and took off on my BMX.

When I got there Natalie was waiting for me, sitting on a curb by the back-door exit ramp. Her brown hair was in a ponytail and she was wearing a sweatshirt that said "Jesus Loves Nazarenes." In jeans with no lipstick, she looked about my age.

She watched me wheel in. Her smile changed me into a white knight, my dirt bike into a charger.

"What seems to be the trouble, ma'am?" I said as I dismounted, surprised to hear myself sound like Troy imitating John Wayne. Her laugh bubbled out.

We bent over her bike and I pushed in on the front tire. Her diagnosis was right on.

"Your mother said I should call you. She says you're a genius with bikes. Is that true?"

"I *wish!*"

Natalie watched while I took off the tire, found the puncture, sanded and patched and checked the tube. I ran my fingers inside the tire itself, hoping for thorns instead of glass, but I didn't find either.

While I ran to the end of the block to get air, Natalie went inside and bought us granola-fig bars from the vending machine. I came back, tightened the axle nuts, spun the wheel. When I finished I wiped my hands off on the grass.

Afterward, it seemed nice just to sit there cross-legged under the Russian olive tree with Natalie and munch health bars.

"We never find time to talk anymore, Buddy," she said. "This place is a zoo."

"Yeah." I stretched out on the grass and looked up at her. "Have you put anything in the B and W can lately?" I was referring to our secret Best and Worst List that we kept all summer. I used to love going down to the laundry to see what new Best or Worst Natalie had added.

"Let's see," she said. "What's happened around here?" When she remembered, she let out a groan. "Yesterday!

Oh, brother! Janice ordered a hundred dollars' worth of silk flowers from Grayson Floral. You know, for the Ladies' Auxiliary Tea? I nearly died. She had them all cut and arranged before anyone saw the invoice."

"Oh my gosh! Who's going to pay for them?"

"Sunnyside, I guess. The director yelled at me for two hours. It's all my fault, you know?" Natalie folded and refolded her cellophane wrapper, her forehead in a knot. "I was sure Smitty would put me on probation again, but she didn't."

"You're the best aide around here, that's why."

"Afraid not, Buddy. But it makes me mad. Here we get Janice so she has some self-respect again—" Suddenly she grinned. "Honest, I wish you'd seen the way they flipped out in the front office."

When I told her our Worst list was now longer than our Best list, she got serious again. "You're right. Something good better happen around here soon."

I stood up to see if her tire was still holding air, when a big black limo pulled up and slid in next to the ten-speed. It was a hearse.

A man in a business suit got out and nodded to Natalie and me. He headed up the ramp just as Gary, the new therapist with the reddish beard, started a stretcher through the double doors above us.

"Come on," Natalie said, springing to her feet, "let's get out of here."

"It's okay," I told her, but it wasn't really. I'd already started breathing hard.

We got on our bikes, and I followed Natalie across the parking lot and out to the street. Waiting there for traffic, Natalie told me she was sorry I had to get in on that . . . and because of her, too.

"Who died?" I asked.

She ran her hands over the yellow wrap on her handlebars. "Nanny Henderson. On East. Did you know her?"

I nodded and felt my eyes start to water. Nanny was blind. From diabetes. She once had me dial a phone number for her at the nurses' station.

I jumped when I heard the back doors of the hearse slam shut. You'd think they'd try to be quiet.

"It's a blessing, really," Natalie said. "There wasn't anything left of her."

Blessing! I stared at her. Since when was dying a blessing?

"Beat you to the stoplight!" Natalie shouted, up on her bike and pumping. I took off, throwing all 116 pounds onto my pedals. I knew Natalie wanted me *gone* before Nanny went by on her way to the mortuary.

CHAPTER
·6·

You'd think the soccer coach would have given up on me long ago. I hadn't gone to practice yet. But no, he kept right on sending me these threatening messages.

"I'm gonna break Tom's butt," he told Jim Needham, so Jim would have the pleasure of passing it on. Or, "I'm gonna kick that kid in the radiator!" I began to think my anatomy was in danger and wondered where it would all end. Naturally, I was still staying out of Mr. Thurston's way after school.

I could no longer avoid Carmela, however, because Mrs. Henessey put us on the Halloween committee together.

"How come you're mad at me?" Carmela asked as we left the building after our first planning meeting.

"I'm not mad at you."

"You act like it."

"Heck, you've been walking to school with Kim Phillips," I said lamely.

"I know, but you were mad before that."

I scattered leaves with my feet, wishing she'd lay off. How could I tell her I was still embarrassed about taking her to the nursing home? How could I tell her that that afternoon was a bigger disappointment for me than it was for her?

"Are you going to Sunnyside right now?" she asked, like she was reading my mind.

"Yep."

"I really had a nice time that day."

"Yeah, sure."

"I did. It was interesting. I'd never been to an old folks' home before."

I thought about Charles, twenty-four and paralyzed from a motorcycle accident, and Cassie, in her thirties, with a bone disease. Nobody calls them "old folks' homes" anymore, doesn't Carmela know that?

We walked along beside each other, both kind of stiff-acting.

"Someone died last week," I blurted out. Recklessly I added, "I saw the hearse come after the body."

She made a horrified face.

"See?" I pounced. "You can't take that stuff. You live in the regular world. I don't. I like it over there where people are crippled up and crabby and . . . and the place smells funny."

"Tom!" She spun me around. "What's wrong with you? I think it's great that you help out at Sunnyside. Honest."

I searched her face, wishing I knew how to say what I was thinking. "Come on—the truth. You think someone would have to be weird to hang around a nursing home."

"I do not! I don't think you're weird at all. Weird is *weird!* Being different is okay. I wish *I* had something to do after school. How would you like it if you had to be home alone every day . . . and your mom and dad . . . didn't show up until six?"

"Okay," I said, throwing a test at her, "if you hate being home alone so much, why don't you come with me right now? Roger's been wanting to meet you. I know he'll be awake this time."

I watched as her face grew red. "You know I can't tonight. I promised I'd have the crepe paper measured and ruffled by tomorrow."

She sounded so sincere I found myself smiling with relief.

"Look, I'm having this great idea," I said. "Why don't I come over to your house after dinner and help you torture the crepe paper? You want me to? Then you could do both."

"Okay." She smiled back and tossed her hair like nothing was ever wrong between us. "I'll have to call Mama, though."

I slid my hands in the rear pockets of my jeans to keep me earthbound. "There are fourteen phones at Sunnyside," I said. "I counted them once." I felt like breaking away and running, I was so excited.

"Remember Laura-the-Kisser?" I asked as we crossed Seventeenth. "Guess what?"

"What?" Carmela giggled.

"She grabbed and kissed two state inspectors yesterday."

Somehow we ended up laughing about Laura all the way to the nursing home.

Not only was Roger awake when we got there, he was making the announcements on the intercom as we walked in. Ever since summer when he was a big hit announcing the Senior Olympics Wheelchair Race, he'd been the official Voice of Sunnyside. By the tone of his "Now hear this!" I figured something big was going on.

"Out of your sacks, mates." The words warbled out deep and mellow. "This is your captain speaking. The old skipper himself is here to invite all you able-bodied seamen—oh, and ladies, too!—to an ice-cream social. Three flavors today. Come right on down to the dining room."

"What?" Roger asked someone in a quiet voice. (He was being prompted.) "Oh, yes—" His announcer's voice floated out again. "FOUR O'CLOCK, MATES! Eight bells, to the initiated. That's ten measly minutes from now. Roll those chariots o' yours right down to the dining room."

When Carmela finished making her call, we hurried on to the social director's office, where I knew we'd find Roger.

Janice, who liked parties as much as flower arranging, was rolling along ahead of us. She looked pretty sporty in her hunter's orange leg-warmers. I tapped her shoulder as Carmela and I parted and sailed around her wheelchair. "Going for ice cream?" I asked.

"I certainly am."

Roger was sitting at the mike table with Mrs. Purdy when we arrived, holding the white captain's hat Natalie bought him. He never made the announcements with it on, like it would be disrespectful or something if he did.

I pushed into the room ahead of Carmela and gave him a smart salute. "Aye, aye, sir."

He swiped at my legs with his cap. "Might have known you'd show up for ice cream, you young scamp. Come here," he growled.

He popped the captain's hat onto my head, adjusted it to suit himself, gave me a look that was as good as a hug.

"Want to assemble that mizzenmast after the party?" he asked.

"Oh!" I whirled around, remembering Carmela. "This is Carmela, Roger. I told you about her." I stepped aside so they could see each other.

"Of course. And the last name?"

"Rice," I said.

Roger leaned on his cane and the edge of the table to stand up, then bowed from the waist as if she was some great lady he was meeting.

I was surprised when Carmela stepped forward and put out her hand, but I guess she was remembering Janice.

"It's a great pleasure," Roger said. I was scared for a minute that he was going to kiss her hand, but he didn't.

"Carmelita, eh? *Hablas español?*"

"*Sí,*" she answered. "*A veces en casa. Y usted?*"

"*Hablo poquito como tú.* Only what a sea captain picks up carrying cargo to Spanish ports . . . *los puertos hispanos.*"

Carmela laughed happily as I looked from one to the other. Roger's face had turned a grandfatherly pink; Carmela's was wide with smiles. I felt about as needed as a cold breeze at a Baskin-Robbins.

"May I interrupt all this?" Mrs. Purdy asked as she went ahead and interrupted. "I'm so shorthanded today I'm losing my mind. Could you kids bring wheelchairs over from East? There isn't a volunteer on the premises except Brett Lovelace, and he's in there dipping ice cream."

I looked at Roger.

"Go on, go on. The lady's shorthanded. You help the old folks. I'll get there under my own steam."

As Carmela and I moved off down the hall, I threw Roger's cap in the air and caught it again. *Captain Tom Palmer*, I said to myself. The words had a nice, salty taste. Then I stuck the cap on Carmela's head so she could wear it awhile.

"Let's get Lucky Lucy first," I said. "She's a real character. She and I have been cooking up escape plans for years. Of course, we never get any further than the courtyard, but she says running away keeps her perkin'."

Carmela laughed, her shiny hair swinging like in the TV ads, and I felt luckier than even Lucy.

When we got to the east hall, we found Lucy's roommate, Agnes, blocking the way. She couldn't get her wheelchair between a laundry rack and the wall, and she was having a fit. I moved the rack and swung her free. "Maybe we should take her to the dining room first," I told Carmela.

"You want me to while you go get Lucy?"

I hesitated. Agnes wasn't the easiest person to help.

"I can do it," Carmela assured me.

"Okay," I agreed and could hear her introducing herself as I took off.

Three seconds later, I was swinging into Lucy's room.

"Oh boy, where we goin'?" she asked as soon as she saw me.

"We're going to sea," I whispered close to her face. "You and Carmela and me . . . we're going to sea!"

"Goodie." She tossed her knitting on the bed *so fast*. "I haven't been to sea since Friday."

I flopped down the wheelchair footrests, lifted her toothpick legs, put her feet on the metal platforms. "Keep your elbows in today, the harbor's full of boats." She laughed and tucked her arms in to her sides.

Coming out of Lucy's, we faced what was Nanny Henderson's old room. It suddenly hit me that her name was gone from the ID plate. Right off I got a prickly feeling in my armpits. That was all that was left of her, and now the name was gone, too.

I picked up my speed with the wheelchair when I saw Carmela ahead, but I couldn't get rid of the prickly sensation or the sad feeling about Nanny.

It was a good thing I hurried. I reached Carmela just in time to save her from Agnes, whose fists were shooting out every which way.

"Lord God in heaven, girl, what are you doing to me?" Her lap robe was tangled in the spokes and her tennis shoes were braking against the floor.

"She won't keep her feet up!" Carmela cried, looking scared and mad at the same time.

"Come on now, cooperate," I said firmly.

When I bent down to get her feet on the rests, she kicked me a good one on the shinbone. "Ow! Agnes!"

"There'll be worse! Don't fool with me, you hear?"

"Okay, okay!"

I'd never seen her so mad. She looked really wired, her eyes darting quick as lightning between us. I glanced around for Natalie, for anyone, but we were all alone in the hall.

Then Carmela bent down and asked her in a voice lots sweeter than I'd have used, "Can you get to the dining room by yourself, Agnes?"

"I always do, don't I? Lord! Get away, both of you!"

Carmela had tears in her eyes when she looked at me again. I shrugged, grinned, felt like taking a dive into the laundry chute.

"You want to push Lucky Lucy?" I asked as we went on, but she shook her head no. When she jammed Roger's hat on my head with enough force to dislodge my ears, I got the idea she was as mad as Agnes.

"She gets these spells," I said, trying to smooth things over. "The trouble is, you never know when. Natalie says not to pay any attention. She doesn't mean anything personal by it."

Carmela looked straight ahead, her mouth and chin in a firm line.

She'll never come back to Sunnyside, I told myself with a sinking heart.

I'd never have the nerve to ask her again, either.

CHAPTER ·7·

I knew as soon as I woke up that the day was special, though I couldn't for the life of me remember why. What day was it? Sunday? Good, no school. No soccer worries. I lay there half-awake, my head full of fuzz, wondering if I could hold out until the season was over after Thanksgiving.

I opened my eyes to look at my dream yacht hanging directly overhead, then saw Roger's face appear as if by magic against the ceiling. Roger! I leaped out of bed. Roger and Natalie were coming to our house for dinner. The first time. Mom was making roast beef and Yorkshire pudding, Roger's favorite. I couldn't dress fast enough once I remembered.

It blew me away that Mom didn't get mad when I invited Roger without asking her first. All she said was "Good. We'll have Natalie, too. That girl's thin as a toothpick. I worry about her living alone in that dumpy little apartment."

For once I didn't complain as Mom and I worked all

morning. We chopped celery and red peppers, ran the vacuum, flipped the feather duster over the pictures and lamps (as if Roger cared if our light bulbs were dusty).

"Can you believe I'd invite company for Sunday dinner when I cook all week long for a living?" Mom asked. She laughed as she whipped a cloth into place on the table. "Tom, dear, remind me to talk to Dr. Grogan about this strange behavior of mine."

Later on, Mom left me in charge of smelling the roast while she took the car to pick up Natalie at her place and Roger at Sunnyside. I went out with the clippers to get some bright orange pyracantha clusters from the hedge. My homemade centerpiece didn't look anything like one of Janice's, but it was colorful.

Then I waited in the living room reading Sunday comics until I heard the squeak of Mom's brakes, at which time the butterflies in my stomach got serious.

Natalie was beaming when she walked in. She'd already been to church and was still dressed up. When she hooked me around the neck and said, "Hi, Buddy, was this your idea?" I noticed she smelled like a bouquet of flowers.

Roger followed her in wearing a white shirt, tie, and a red vest with only two visible spots on it. He hooted when I told him he looked like the teller at American Savings and Loan.

Pretty soon we sat down at the table and started passing around the good food Mom fixed. We ate. We talked about things. Nothing important, just things families talk about at Sunday dinners. Mom and Natalie had to gossip about certain people they didn't like on the staff, and

Roger threw in his two bits' worth when he wasn't talking to me. I kept thinking about Troy and wishing he were home with us again.

It all went too fast. By two o'clock the meal was over except for the lemon pie and coffee we were going to have later.

Roger shook his head. "I can't believe we finished that big roast in one sitting. You're puttin' food away like a longshoreman, Buddy."

"Me!" I sat up straight. "It was you and Natalie."

Natalie laughed and poked me, after which we did a little slapping under the table—until Mom gave me the eye and Natalie quit.

After suggesting that Roger and I go catch some rays outside, Mom went upstairs and brought down a sweater that had belonged to my dad. She helped Roger put it on, then buttoned it up part way. He stood there straight and still, seemed to enjoy having her fuss. As he worked his shoulders and tried the pockets, I tried to imagine how he'd look in a ship captain's uniform.

"Well, ma'am," he told Mom a minute later, "that was a dinner fit for the gods. Never had such good company, either."

Mom broke into a big smile. "It would be a pure joy what I do, if everyone had your appetite, young man. And your manners!"

Suddenly they were giving each other these big hugs— my short, cushiony mom and tall, skinny old Roger. I grinned like crazy, feeling the way kids do in families where there's a dad and lots of teasing around.

Then the two of us went on out to the back yard. Roger asked me if I'd planted the tulip bulbs yet, and I showed him where I dug up the ground alongside the garage. I pulled some straggly Concord grapes off our vines and gave him a bunch so we'd have something to do in the glider.

Sitting there, I could hear the sounds from inside—pans banging against the sink, silverware clinking. I felt very peaceful. I think Roger felt peaceful, too, because he wasn't talking. We just rocked back and forth and spit seeds over the tips of our shoes. I felt him shiver once. "That sun's mighty weak," he said finally, "but it's all we got."

"Yep. Winter's coming."

He popped another grape into his mouth. "I wouldn't mind winter at all if I was a working man. You live in Newfoundland half your life, you don't worry about the cold.

"Over there"—he nodded in the direction of Sunny-side"—it's eighty degrees year round, enough to dry up a man's gizzard and everything else."

"I guess you hate being retired, huh?"

"I didn't think it would turn out this way. Thought I'd always live where I could smell the kelp . . . hear the roar of the sea."

Picking up his cane, he pointed toward the west. "Look over there." We could see the Oquirrh Mountain Range from where we sat, the peaks already dusted with snow. "And there." His angry sweep of the foothills to the east was enough to make them disappear.

"LANDLOCKED!" he roared, the word shooting out as if from a cannon.

I must have jumped, because he put a hand on my leg and patted me back into place.

I didn't say anything, but I couldn't blame him for feeling mad and disappointed. His only daughter checked him into the nursing home, then moved to Arizona when her husband was transferred. Roger's other kid, who has a big tourist business in the Greek islands (with a yacht named *Miz Blu*), was supposed to relocate Roger in Newfoundland. He hadn't gotten around to it yet.

"Gaylen won't quit while there's money to be made," Roger told me once. "I'll probably die here. The old ticker's got its limits."

His voice sounded just as sad now when he said, "Some days, Buddy, I stretch out on my bed and just leave that little cell. I watch those sails go up . . . and fill . . . Other times it's the booms I hear, startin' to squeak. The wind dies out, and the rolling gets so gentle a baby wouldn't notice it. We end up in a flat calm and I know nothing's going to happen for awhile—"

He paused, then looked off. "That's the way I put myself to sleep when time gets heavy on my hands."

"I'll never have as interesting a life as you," I told him, tossing my empty grape stalk. "I know I won't."

Roger leaned against my shoulder. I thought he was showing me how he put himself to sleep, so I laughed and made a comical snore.

He slumped heavier. Suddenly I realized his whole weight was against me.

What's wrong? I tried pushing him back up, but I couldn't, and his eyes were empty.

"Mom," I screamed. "Get out here!"

His mouth was sagging and his head lolled toward me. His saliva smeared my cheek as I struggled to get my arms around him.

"Mom . . . Roger!" I screamed again, but she was right there behind the glider, straightening him. Natalie was there, too, pulling my arm away so she could lift his face. His eyes were filled with fog, and my heart was beating right out of my chest.

"Looks like a stroke," Natalie said. "Bring up the car. We can get him over there in two minutes. He may need oxygen."

"Oh, dear God!" Mom ran to the house for her keys.

By the time she had the car going, Roger seemed to be coming back. He blinked, moaned, but he was so limp you could tell something had happened.

Somehow we got him on his feet and half-carried him to the car, maneuvering him into the front seat. Natalie got into the back and leaned over his shoulder to hold him up.

"Tom," she shouted. "Call Sunnyside. Tell them to get Dr. Grogan. Say it's an emergency."

"And then stay home!" Mom yelled sharply as she backed off the grass and down the drive.

I whirled away and headed for the phone. No way was I going to stay at home while Roger was having a stroke. I thought of Nanny. But Roger wasn't weak or sick—he was strong! His grip—it was something you wouldn't believe.

I pushed the buttons for Sunnyside, then watched the

whole kitchen go blurry. I got Smitty on and told her what happened, but my voice was shaking so bad I could hardly get out the words.

"Don't worry," she said in a rush, "we'll meet him at the door."

I stood at the kitchen sink awhile, wiping my face on a tea towel. I didn't know what to do. The house was deadly quiet. I thought about how we all sat around the table laughing, how spiffy Roger looked, how happy we were.

"Mom, I'm not staying here!" I said aloud. I grabbed my jacket from the hook on the back porch and headed for my bike. In three minutes I was at Sunnyside.

Mom and Natalie were standing in the hall outside Roger's room talking—waiting for Dr. Grogan, I soon learned. I knew they wouldn't let me past their barricade. Mom put her arm around me, but I turned my face away.

The nursing home had a Sunday quiet, a kind of visitor-hum as people talked in low voices. Suddenly I hated all that quiet. I wanted to hear the intercom blasting and the carts rattling. I wanted things to be normal— plain everyday normal!

"I hope it isn't his heart," Natalie said softly to Mom.

"Will he be okay?" I asked when nobody told me anything. My squeaky voice gave away how scared I was.

Natalie grabbed up my hand and squeezed it between hers. "Oh, Buddy, he's very old."

A male orderly came down the hall rolling an oxygen tank. Smitty met him at the door, the stethoscope on her neck. They went back in, hurrying, but I shifted around and got a glimpse of Roger. He was lying there so still in his red vest I wanted to choke.

I pulled away and ran down the hall to an exit. I couldn't stay there at his room . . . but I couldn't go home either. . . .

I got on my bike and started riding, counterclockwise, on the drive that encircled the nursing home.

I passed Roger's window and could see Smitty bending over him.

Around again.

The next time Natalie was in there with Smitty.

Finally, Dr. Grogan.

Another dozen times and I saw Mom come out of the kitchen delivery door wearing Dad's sweater. I doubled back and rode alongside the lilac hedge until I heard her drive away.

I don't know why, but I got this idea that if I kept pedaling, Roger would keep on living. It was like I was giving him some of my strength, like my legs were pumping oxygen out of that tank into his lungs.

I kept going, around and around.

I didn't stop even when Natalie came out and tried to make me. I didn't stop when it got dark, either, and it started spitting rain. I wouldn't have stopped all night long if Mom hadn't driven back over and threatened to call the police on me.

CHAPTER
·8·

When I woke up the next morning, Mom was already gone and it was a quarter to eight. There was a note propped against the toaster: "I called Sunnyside and Roger's still alive. Try not to worry."

I blasted out of the house with a slice of peanut-butter toast in my hand. I was plenty late. After all that cycling the night before, my legs were screaming, but I ran all the way anyhow. At the last minute—knowing I couldn't gag it down—I chucked my toast to the yellow dog begging in front of the junior high.

The day didn't get any better as it went along. In English, our only class together, Carmela tried to pass me a note. It got intercepted. Mrs. Henessey then glared at me instead of her. I kept looking back at Carmela, but she never got her message across to me. I wanted to tell her about Roger in the worst way, but when Mrs. Henessey asked her to stay after class I knew I wouldn't have a chance.

On top of everything else, I'd gone off and left my math assignment home. Fourteen story problems—an hour's worth of homework—trapped inside my math book on the floor of my room.

My mind just slid away as Mr. Olivetti went on and on about decimals and percentages. I remembered what happened in the glider the day before, and my heart got to pounding exactly the way it did then. I could feel Roger's shoulder slumping against me. I could see the side of his mouth hanging loose. I wanted to raise my hand and say, "Listen, Mr. Olivetti, I need to know what happens when a person gets a stroke. Is it fatal? Always or sometimes? Is it more fatal when you're old?"

I stared out the window and found myself wishing Troy were home. He sometimes hated my questions, but I could usually get him to answer by pointing out that I didn't have a father to ask about stuff. Lately I'd just been saving my questions for Roger. Last week, when I asked him what happened if you liked two girls, not just one, he said it was okay.

"Like as many as you want, Buddy, but you only marry one at a time. At your age I liked them all. It's natural."

I blinked at the incomprehensible math problem inching its way down the front blackboard and wished I were at Sunnyside.

"Any questions?" Mr. Olivetti asked. He dusted chalk off his hands, then started passing out a quiz. Like Roger said *he* did, I just sailed away on separate seas. Maybe I'd never come back.

I came back, all right, and in the very next class. I couldn't believe my eyes when I walked into gym and found Mr. Thurston there instead of our regular gym teacher. He was holding the almighty clipboard, which meant he was substituting that period.

I figured he didn't know me yet by sight . . . maybe I could sneak out before roll . . . *Oh, lord, too late!* He shooed the whole bunch of us into the dressing room before I could make my move.

"Five minutes!" he yelled. "Everyone on the floor and running in five. Get the lead out, Cramer," he said to someone he knew.

I had good reason to worry. My name on the roll rang every bell in Mr. Thurston's head.

"Stand up, Palmer," he ordered me. "I want to get a look at you."

I managed to stand, but my legs wavered like seaweed.

"Come up here."

I stepped over John, worked my way between Jason and the grinning hyena sitting next to him. Row by row, I passed through the bodies, my gym shoes slapping the silence until I found myself face to face with Mr. Thurston's incredible sneer.

He looked me up and down, turned me around with one finger. With everyone's eyes on me, I felt flabby and white-skinned. My ears were on fire, but I kept my mind on the *Cutty Sark* and how Roger and I would use steel wool to make the decks look used.

"Tom Palmer," he said, like my name was vomit in his mouth, "you couldn't play on my soccer team even if you *had* the decency to show up."

"No, sir," I mumbled. "I mean, yes, sir. That's what I told my mom."

"YOUR MOM!"

The gym exploded with howls.

Mr. Thurston looked over my head at the class. "What would you do with a kid who signs up for soccer then never gets his butt to practice?"

"A thousand push-ups!" someone yelled.

My eyes stung.

"A hundred sit-ups!"

They shouted over each other. "Ten times around the school! . . . Twenty! . . . Kick him in the radiator!"

"Aw, leave him alone!" came a voice from the back that nobody heard but me.

The sit-up torture won. Thurston hauled me farther out in front where everyone could see, then told me to start counting.

I began with my hands behind my head, knowing I'd be lucky to reach thirty.

Mercifully, he finished roll before putting the spotlight on me again. "How many, Palmer?"

"Twenty-seven," I said weakly. How would I ever make it? I was so sweaty already I could smell myself.

"Take him to sixty," he told the class, then headed for the gym office to pull absentee cards.

"Twenty-eight," the class chanted as I started in again. "Twenty-nine . . ."

They got louder and faster as we went along. I lowered my arms, but I couldn't keep up. They were loving it. *Loving* it! My neck muscles felt like chains. I could see my belly shaking right through my gym shirt.

"Thirty-nine, forty . . ."

It was all over. I rolled face down on the hardwood

floor, wishing I could cry. I hid my face in my arms. I didn't care what punishment came next.

"Forty-three . . . forty-four . . ." They went right on counting. I took deep breaths and tried not to lose my cool.

"Forty-eight . . . forty-nine . . . fifty . . ."

All of a sudden I realized they were letting me rest. Why were they doing that? Every kid out there—glad it wasn't *him*—was giving me a break!

When they reached fifty-three I started in again. Amazingly, I made it the rest of the way to sixty.

"He did it!" The nice guy at the back jumped to his feet. He got the whole class to clapping. They whistled and shouted. Some rotten kid yelled "Cheat!" but he got a shove from behind. I staggered back to my place, so grateful I gave everyone a bold victory sign. Jim Needham and a bunch of other friends patted me as I stumbled by.

I figured the worst of it was over, but when Thurston came out on the floor again, he couldn't resist one last dig.

"There was a Troy Palmer playing football for Highland last year," he told everyone. "Top-notch quarterback, that kid. When I saw someone with the same last name on the soccer list . . . man, that got my hopes up." He gave me a smile that was supposed to make me feel better, but it didn't.

He finished his speech with "Too bad you're not related to him."

I didn't open my mouth. I just gave him back my laser stare.

It was Jim Needham who figured he ought to set the

record straight. "He *is* related," he shouted. "Troy's his brother."

After school I got to the nursing home in less time than it takes our student body to empty the vending machines. Five minutes at the outside.

I took a big breath when I saw the red stop sign on Roger's door. NO SMOKING, OXYGEN IN USE. He was still alive!

Inside, the drapes were closed, but someone had turned on the trawler lantern that hung by the bathroom door. Its flame-shaped yellow light was the only cheerful thing about room eighteen.

I tiptoed to Roger's bed. His eyes were closed, and he looked whiter than I could ever remember him. There was a tube in his nose and the whole thing was taped onto his face.

I stood there awhile, not making a sound except for swallowing. His chest rose, fell. Very little, just enough to see. I waited. I wished his eyelids would move. Suddenly I had this big urge to pat him, but I couldn't decide where to pat him, and I knew I shouldn't wake him up. I sneaked my hand along the sheet until it was close enough to feel his warmth, and I left it there awhile.

It crossed my mind that Roger could actually die before the *Cutty Sark* was finished. I wouldn't be able to do it alone, it was too hard. I didn't even want to do it without him. Why did he have to get a stroke before we started work on the rigging, anyway?

I let out my breath, knowing I'd give anything to hear him sounding off at the model manufacturers right then.

Light streamed into the room over my shoulder. Natalie came in, checked the gauge on the oxygen tank, then took me into the hall so we could talk.

"I came early today to see if I could get him to take some lunch," she told me, "but other than a few bites of applesauce—"

"Did he say anything?"

"He isn't talking much yet, but his vital signs are stabilizing and that's what counts. He can swallow okay, but he kept pushing my hand away. I think he just didn't want to be fed. He can be stubborn, you know."

"Yeah, I know." We went on talking while we walked to the ice machine.

Suddenly she smiled. "Hey, guess what Dr. Grogan called him."

"What?"

"A tough old turkey."

I smiled, picturing Thanksgiving.

"He said it right to his face. 'You're a tough old turkey,' he said. And I could tell Roger understood him. You know how his mustache always gives him away."

"Yeah."

I helped Natalie fill her ice cart, then gave her a hand doing the water pitchers on West. I couldn't stand sitting in the hold by myself, and I sure didn't want to think about what happened at school.

Later, Mom and I ate dinner in the Sunnyside kitchen, which we did when she needed to stay for a meeting. The high-school kids who came in to serve and clean up were yakking away, but we didn't pay any attention.

I thought about the light snow that had been blowing

all day. I sure hated having things end—the seasons, a good book, Troy living at home. I went into a terrible decline when *M.A.S.H.* was over. I even feel sad throwing away my old toothbrushes, for crying out loud!

"You're awfully quiet tonight," Mom said to me.

I took a bite of cornbread, looked up. "Is Roger going to get well?"

"With someone his age, all you can do is wait and see."

How could she be so calm? Is that what happens when you get old—really old? Everyone just waits for you to die? *Better die now, old dude, your time is up.*

"Wish I could go in and talk to him," I said.

"He needs the rest more than he needs you."

"Why'd he have to have a stupid stroke, anyway? He said he was so spry the other day he might just get on the payroll here."

"For doing what? Baby-sitting you?"

"Nooooo!"

"Tom," she said pretty soon, "don't get too attached to Roger. You know he can't live forever. No one lives forever."

I washed the cornbread down with milk and forced myself to think about Carmela. If I didn't lose my nerve, I was going to call her when I got home.

CHAPTER
·9·

I did get on the phone that night, and it made me feel better to tell Carmela about Roger. I guess I started something, though. The next night after dinner, Carmela called me.

"How was Roger today?" she asked.

"He knew me. He squeezed my hand, called me 'Buddy.' "

The next night I called her. Then she, me. We ended up phoning back and forth for nine whole school days. Even though we walked together every morning, we had a conversation about Roger every night at home. It was kind of neat, but I got the feeling Mom was about to make a proclamation.

"Aren't you carrying this 'Roger Report' a little far?" she finally asked.

Friday night, when it was Carmela's turn to call, I decided to surprise her by getting to the phone first. I waited until Mom was settled in front of the TV with her coffee and paper before I punched out the numbers I'd memorized nearly two weeks ago.

"Hello," Carmela answered.

"This is Doctor Tom Palmer speaking." I deepened my voice. "Would you mark this on Roger's chart, Miss Rice? Captain Ericksen's temperature today was 98.3, his blood pressure was 160 over 115. Glucose was normal. You got it down?"

I expected her to laugh, but there was a big scary silence on the line.

"You still there?" I squeaked.

"How come the girls always have to be the nurses? Mrs. Henessey says—"

"Okay, hold it"—I thought fast—"I'm the nurse making the report and *you're* the doctor. What I mean is . . . you know . . . maybe you're sick of hearing about Roger and would like to go out to a movie or something."

She gasped. "Tom, I'm not allowed to date boys until I'm fifteen. I told you that, remember?

Of course I remembered, why else would I ask?

"Anyway, I like hearing about Roger," she went on. "I made a get-well card for him today in art with all the words in spanish. *¡Que se Mejore!* it says on the front. Do you think he'll like it?"

"Sí, Señorita," I said, using my entire foreign-language vocabulary.

"I glued my picture in it, too. Of course, it's last year's picture from when we lived in Denver and my hair was short."

"Roger asked about you today."

"Really? What'd he say?"

"He said, 'How's your—' " I almost forgot and said *girlfriend,* but caught myself. "—'friend?' "

"He must be talking better."

"Lots better, except he still forgets words. He called his bed a boat the other day. Crazy stuff like that. But his memory's back, and he's up using a wheelchair now. Rolling it one-handed. He told Mom he wanted a rain check on the lemon pie he missed at our house."

"So . . . what did you tell him when he asked about me?"

"I told him your Girl Scout troop was making bibs for Sunnyside residents, and it was all your idea."

"Tom, that's supposed to be a Christmas surprise!"

"Yeah, but Roger said, 'Don't stick any bibs on me!' "

Carmela laughed.

"He's the one who *needs* a bib," I told her. "I tried to feed him some spaghetti tonight, but he wouldn't let me. He got mad and knocked his plate onto the floor. He hasn't forgotten any cuss words, that's for sure!"

I laughed along with Carmela, but what seemed funny talking to her didn't seem so funny when it happened. With his left side partly paralyzed, Roger couldn't do much for himself. Even his right hand shook so bad food went flying everywhere when he ate. Watching him made me want to cry.

"What was Natalie doing?" Carmela asked, bringing me back.

"Working. She doesn't dare spend too much time in his room. She got in trouble for giving him a back rub today when she was supposed to be delivering linens. Hey, I want to ask you something." I crossed my fingers in front of my face, knowing Carmela hadn't been to Sunnyside since Agnes hurt her feelings that day.

"So ask me."

"There's going to be a wine-and-cheese hour over there Wednesday afternoon. It's traditional, something they do before Thanksgiving. You want to come with me after school and help? It's pretty fun. There'll be balloons and food and stuff."

"Wine?" she asked. I could see her wrinklng her nose.

"Well, punch for us."

"I don't know." There was this dead silence on the line. "I'll tell you Wednesday, okay? I may have something with the scouts that day."

My voice sounded dead, too, when I said, "Okay, tell me Wednesday."

"Mama says I'm calling you too much, so I'm glad you called first."

I could feel her smile coming right through the phone, and it cheered the socks off me. "Yeah, well . . . me too. Okay, then . . ." Suddenly a phrase came to me from my years of Saturday morning cartoons. "¡Adiós, amigos!" I said with a flourish.

For some reason, that sent Carmela into hysterics. "Amiga, Tom, not amigos. I'm a girl!"

Amigos, amiga? How was I supposed to know? Roger could have taught me some Spanish the last two years if only he'd wanted to.

At the end we both resorted to English. "Bye," we said.

CHAPTER ·10·

It seemed funny to hear the therapist's voice on the intercom instead of Roger's when I walked into Sunnyside after school.

"There will be a Thanksgiving wine-and-cheese hour today," he was saying. "Three-thirty in the dining room."

Ho-hum. Gary's a nice guy, I guess, but he had about as much enthusiasm for making the announcements as I did for playing soccer. The voice coming over the airways since Roger's stroke was definitely *not* our captain speaking.

Gary went on giving instructions, even though the "da-da-da-daaaaa" noises coming from Elaine's room threatened to drown him out. He finished with "We'll be asking what you're thankful for on this holiday, so everyone come prepared."

If "da-da-da" was all you could say, what in the world would you have to be thankful for?

I nearly smashed into Natalie, who was hurrying out of Laura-the-Kisser's room.

"Buddy!" she said. "Where's Carmela?"

"She had to put some pork chops in the oven for her mom. She's coming, though."

"Good." She patted the pocket of her pink uniform as she swung on down the hall. "I've got magic markers right here for both of you."

I was almost at the corner when she called back, "I added something to the B and W list today."

I gave her a thumbs-up sign and hurried on toward West.

I pulled up short at the door marked EMPLOYEES ONLY and took the stairs down to the basement. It had been ages since I'd looked at our Best and Worst list.

I went on through the laundry room with its monster-size washers and dryers, then passed the smoking room, where some of the aides were sitting around. "Hi, Buddy," someone called as I went by. I waved.

We kept our list in a can hidden above the hot water pipes in the grungy part of the basement. Half the time the can was so hot you couldn't touch it with your bare hands. I found a rag, then stood on a chair, rolled the can toward me, and jumped down. When I was sure no one had heard me, I sat back to read what Natalie had added to our collection.

I figured she'd had some big disaster again, so I started with the back of the sheet where we'd written our Worsts, but the last sentence was about Roger: "Roger had a stroke today at the Palmers'. I'm so worried about him! Please, God, give him peace."

I looked up and stared at a crack branching out over the concrete wall, remembering how scared we were that afternoon. I wondered, too, why Natalie would write "give him peace." I studied her handwriting on the page. The "Please, God" was shaky, all right. "Don't let him die!" was what I was praying over and over.

I turned the paper over and sighed with relief to see that the Bests had definitely got ahead of the Worsts.

"I called the *Deseret News*," read Best #11. "They're coming out to take Glen's picture because of his 95th birthday and that formal white card he got from the president. He asked if I'd get him a new tie before the photographer got here, so I went through the lost-and-found. Came up with a gorgeous silk one. Glen said it was sexy."

I chuckled, wondering what makes a brown-and-pink tie sexy. The colors didn't even show up in the newspaper.

#12. "Adele Harriman walked to the end of Main, and back. She gets to go home to her apartment Saturday."

#13. "Hooray, hooray! Dory brushed her teeth by herself and got her partial plate back in RIGHT SIDE UP!!!! She's making progress. Didn't I tell you, Buddy?"

I laughed as I reached in the can for the warm ballpoint. It had just popped into my head that I had a Best of my own to add. It was something Roger said yesterday when I found his pipe for him: "When in the (censored) are we going to get back to work on the *Cutty Sark*?" It didn't look like much in writing, but I thought it was the best Best on the list.

The wine-and-cheese party was already under way

when I got back upstairs, though there were still a few stragglers in the hall.

Charles was there, the guy in his twenties who had the terrible motorcycle accident. He loved happy hour better than anyone, I think. Propped up behind the scaffolding fixed to his wheelchair, he actually seemed to enjoy himself at parties. I bent down, gave him a big grin, then watched as his face lit up. Being a quadriplegic doesn't mean you don't know what's going on, that's for sure.

I looked around for Carmela, but so far there was no sign of her. Cody and Brooke, a couple of other volunteers, were at the serving table squirting cheese on crackers and setting out paper cups. We talked a minute.

"Where have you been?" Mom asked as she came up and grabbed me from behind. She kissed me on the head. "I thought you'd be first in line. Did Carmela decide not to come?"

"She'll be here," I answered like a broken record.

"Listen, Tom, I have some errands to run, so you go straight home after this is over. Fix some nachos to hold you 'til I get there, okay?"

"Okay," I said, thinking, *Good idea! Maybe Carmela will stop by and have a bowl of nachos with me.*

After Mom left, Mrs. Purdy came in with the box of colored balloons I helped stamp. GIVING THANKS AT SUNNYSIDE they said. She wore one floating up from the back of her belt. In her handwriting, it said, "Nina Purdy is thankful for her job!"

The residents sitting around at the tables didn't act very thankful or very patient, either. Evaline-the-Cusser was already grumbling. I never knew anyone to be so hungry. Three times a day she bolted for the dining room in her walker, bolted down her food, bolted out again. The high-school kids working in the kitchen made bets on how fast she could polish off a meal.

Richard and Mr. Lorenzo, who always insisted on sitting together, were going at it like cats and dogs. What a pair! If Richard said the soup was hot, Mr. Lorenzo said it was cold. They didn't even look at each other when they fought. What fun could it be?

Before I could get across the dining room to where Roger was sitting, Natalie snagged me. "Can you do the writing on the balloons for us? Gary's coming with the helium right now."

She took a felt-tip pen out of her pocket and handed it to me. "Do you mind? I'll help write, too, if Carmela doesn't get here."

I opened the pen, sniffed it. "What am I supposed to write?"

"Anything. Mrs. Purdy wants us to say what we're thankful for."

Mrs. Purdy was already at the mike explaining. "After the party," she was saying, "we'll set our balloons free in the courtyard. Your messages will float out over the city for others to find tomorrow—our national holiday for giving thanks. Who knows"—she said, making with the big eyes—"our balloons may get as far as Kansas City. Wouldn't that be something?"

"Mine's going to Chicago!" Glen insisted, stomping the floor with his cane. I pictured an upper airflow chart and what it would take.

I waited while Gary filled balloons and Natalie tied on the strings, but I kept looking across at the door. Every time someone came in I thought it was Carmela. *How long does it take to put three pork chops in the oven?*

The other aides were starting around with the snack crackers and the wine bottles. "Red or white?" they'd ask. "Diabetics get punch."

"Just pour it," Evaline growled.

"I'll have a taste of the Beaujolais," Janice said politely when the wine came to her table.

"Beaujolais!" the aide hooted. "Don't we wish!"

Natalie handed me another filled balloon and told me I'd better get started, with or without Carmela, so I did.

I began with Juanita, who'd been watching us. She looked like one of those Cabbage Patch dolls whose eyes get lost in their fat cheeks.

"What are you thankful for, Juanita?"

Wouldn't you know, she started crying! I figured that meant she wasn't thankful for anything, but then she surprised me. "Mama," she said between sobs. She lifted her flowered skirt and wiped her nose on it. I patted her shoulder, pulled her dress back down when she was through mopping up.

"What's her name?" I asked like a dolt. (Juanita couldn't remember her own name.) Quickly I added, "Shall I just write 'Mama' on your balloon?"

She nodded. I told her I was thankful for my mom, too. I tied the string of the balloon to her wheelchair, then bobbed it up and down for her. I also told her she looked pretty with her new hair-do and finally got her smiling.

I went on around the table. The next person asked me

to write "Medicare." Evaline, naturally, said "Food." Several said they were thankful for their grandchildren. Janice, who never got married, was thankful for her eyesight. I spelled it eye*site*, but Smitty, who stopped to see how I was doing, said, "Leave it, I like it that way." Lucy had me draw a four-leaf clover on hers, and then she showed it to everyone.

It took forever to get to Roger. He'd already finished his wine by the time I reached his table.

"Hi, Roger," I said, grabbing his hand up off the wheelchair. "How you doing today?"

He smiled a little, but he shook his head from side to side.

"Not so good?"

I sat down on the window ledge beside him. Natalie brought over enough balloons for the whole table, and Roger held the strings while I wrote on them. The pen made squeaking sounds and the ink smelled like medicine, but I was the only one who seemed to notice.

Glen said he was thankful for the president, who sent him the birthday card. Beside him old Jacob, who'd been giving the government heck every day of his life at Sunnyside, had me write "our fascist police state" on his.

"Go on, put it down, I'll spell it for you," he said when I hesitated.

According to Mom, Jacob's ongoing quarrel with the government was all that kept him alive. At ninety-eight he was still fighting "the takeover."

"Buddy," Roger said when I'd done every balloon but his, "if you could wet this old sailor's whistle one more time, I'd be more thankful than I am right now." He shoved his paper cup toward me with his good hand, and I motioned to the aide who was making the rounds.

By the wall clock it was already a quarter to five.

Carmela isn't coming. She said she would, but she's not. I glanced out the window. Half an hour more and it would be getting dark.

Once Roger had his wine, I asked him what he was thankful for besides his refill.

"Write 'Buddy' on there," he said, in a voice that sounded almost like the old Roger. So I did, in great big letters.

Then I got myself a balloon and wrote "Roger" on it. We traded pokes, and I tied them on both arms of his wheelchair.

Too bad, Carmela, I'll bet I'm having more fun than you are!

When we finally finished with the balloon writing, I sat down by Roger to drink my punch. I ate some crackers and cheese while Mrs. Purdy recited "Over the River and Through the Woods." Roger sniffed a few times, and I guessed he was remembering better Thanksgivings he'd had.

My mind turned to what Mom and I were planning. Our holiday wouldn't be a big deal with Troy gone. Mom said she'd take me to a movie after dinner if she wasn't too tired—and I supposed we'd call Troy long distance and talk awhile.

My first Thanksgiving without my brother! It wouldn't be much fun. I remembered last year when his girlfriend and a bunch of teammates came over to watch the Nebraska-Oklahoma game. Mom and I practically killed ourselves serving snacks and hot cider to that crowd. But it was great. I sighed, wondering how Troy would spend the holiday so far away from home.

Maybe I'd just take Roger to the hold tomorrow. He could watch while I worked. For three weeks, all I'd done on our model was paint the rub rail and stare at the flag assortment. It was no fun building the *Cutty Sark* alone.

Pretty soon the aides started taking people out into the courtyard, two or three at a time, where Natalie would snip the strings. They'd watch the balloons take off, then everyone got rushed back in where it was warm. Some of the residents preferred to watch from inside, but they all seemed excited to be sending messages to the "outside world."

When it was Roger's turn he insisted on going out, anyway, in his shirtsleeves. "There you go, Buddy," he said, giving his balloon a salute.

I broke mine loose and ran with it a few steps. "There you go, Roger, catching up with me!"

"Free at last," he said, "riding on the wind."

The same wind lifted the hairs on the back of his head and made him shiver.

In the chilly light, I noticed how much skinnier he looked and how much smaller. He asked to stay out, but a minute later he was clutching his bad arm to his chest and shaking so hard I hurried to get him back inside.

"We could go work on the *Sark*," I told him, putting on the cheer as we cruised along to the men's wing. "You want to? It's always nice and warm in there."

"Take me home," he said, "I'm tired."

I let my face collapse, glad he couldn't see me behind

the wheelchair. Suddenly, I felt old and tired, too. In fact, I felt awesomely old and awesomely tired. I said goodbye, promising I'd be back for Thanksgiving, then started on home.

Without a cap or gloves or anything, I got a good case of the shakes myself. The temperature was dropping. I figured there'd be snow by morning.

By the time I reached home I knew I wouldn't call Carmela. If she didn't call me, it would be all over between us.

"Maybe it's all over, anyway," I said to myself in a dismal voice.

CHAPTER
·11·

I missed my whole Thanksgiving vacation by being sick in bed with the flu. Even Sunday, when I started feeling better, Mom wouldn't let me go near Sunnyside for fear I'd spread germs around. I ended up staring at the telephone, trying to make it ring, and wishing I had the *Cutty Sark* home so I could work on it.

I got so bored with TV I finally broke away and read a book Mom brought me from the library Saturday. *Captain Harry Thomasen: Forty Years At Sea.* It was a great account of this skipper's life on the old-timey schooners. Roger could have written it himself.

When I got tired of reading and sipping chicken soup, I found a clean sheet of notebook paper and wrote a note to Natalie.

"Put this down as a 'Worst,' " it began. "Tom was sick for four long, miserable days!!!"

I also asked her to please explain to Roger why I

couldn't come over. I ended with a riddle for her amusement: "How did the chicken wearing purple swim-fins drown in the duck pond?" It was a made-up riddle with no answer, but I knew Natalie would suffer over it.

I went to school Monday morning with my nose plugged and my ears ringing, but there was nothing wrong with my eyes. I sure enough saw Carmela in English, but I acted as if I didn't. I sailed right past her desk. Then I jumped into Mrs. Henessey's prepositions like they were the most interesting parts of speech ever studied at John Glenn Junior High.

Later, when I noticed Carmela coming toward my table at lunch, I quickly turned my head and started a conversation. "How'd the soccer season end up?" I asked Jim Needham, who still ate with me most days.

He was happy as a fly in a pudding dish, giving me a goal-by-goal account of the final game. I only half-listened, but it kept Carmela from stopping and making excuses for not coming to the Thanksgiving party.

It was the next Saturday afternoon before Mom would let me visit Sunnyside again. I was so glad to see Roger that we had to do an arm wrestle as soon as I walked into his room. I could tell he was weaker than I was, so I let him win, then I worried if it was *seeing* me or *beating* me that perked him up most. It didn't matter. The great thing was, he seemed a whole lot better.

"Know what I'd like to do today?" he asked me right off the bat.

"You want to work on the *Sark*, I'll bet."

"Well, we need to get on her again, that's for sure, but today"— he glanced at the window—"that sun feels mighty good. Might be our last chance to go to the greenhouse. Is it too cold outside for an old geezer?"

"No, it's nice out there. Let's go, that'll be fun." My mind raced ahead, wondering how he'd feel having me push him around the greenhouse in a wheelchair, when he'd always walked before.

I slid open the closet door and looked for his coat. "You going to buy today, or are we just looking?"

"Both," he said, "you'll see." I put my own woolly cap on Roger and wound a scarf around his neck. He asked for his pipe, put it in his mouth. He didn't want the tobacco pouch, which made me wonder if Smitty had caught on to him.

I told Natalie where we were going, but I didn't waste time getting anyone else's permission. I just pushed open that wide front door with my rear end, and out we rolled.

"Don't suppose we'll be going by a tobacco shop," Roger joked as we bumped across the parking lot. I wished one would spring up right in front of us on the asphalt. I had Roger's ten bucks in my pocket. I'd go in and get him a bag of Black Lung or something and let him have the smoke he was craving. To heck with Smitty!

The lady at the checkout counter gave us a surprised look. "My two best customers! Where have you been? How are you, Roger?"

He whipped my cap off his head, smoothed his few hairs. "I'm pert enough . . . for an old buzzard who's had his wings clipped."

She laughed, then shook her head and looked sorry. She went on staking up her philodendron, but I knew she felt bad to see Roger being pushed around like an invalid. He just stuck out his chin and made an impatient motion for us to get on with it.

We started at the front of the greenhouse where dozens of little pine trees had been put into pots to sell. LIVING CHRISTMAS TREES, the sign said, and there was every variety you could think of.

Roger clucked his tongue. "Those poor youngsters," he said, as if what we were seeing was a display table full of orphans.

I pushed him around to a dark green pine I recognized on the other side of the table, a little one not two feet tall. I lifted it into Roger's lap.

"I know what this is," I said. "It's a Monterey pine."

"Good, good. A fast-growing Monterey. Remember how big they get?"

"Fifty feet? Taller than this greenhouse, anyway."

"Up to a hundred feet."

I put the Monterey back so he could look at the others.

"Scotch. Lodgepole. I don't see any Bristlecones here," he said, pulling himself along the table. "Did I ever tell you about the Bristlecones?"

I nodded and grinned. *Lots of times!*

"There's a stand of Bristlecone pines in Nevada older than Jesus Christ himself," he told me anyway. "I always wanted to see those granddaddy Bristlecones. Never got there. Can you imagine walking right up to an oldtimer like that and having a conversation?"

"Yeah," I said with a laugh.

We hung around the pines a little more, until Roger was

sure we'd seen and identified everything, then we bumped across the rough floor to the bulb bins. He asked for the third time if I'd put my tulips in the ground.

I thought back to summertime, when the whole greenhouse was ablaze with color, when Roger and I could spend an hour sniffing the roses and honeysuckle and not pay a nickle for the entertainment.

"Never had a garden," Roger said. "A seafaring man has to find his gardens in books. Or in his head."

On the way out, he surprised me by asking the checkout lady for the nicest, fullest Zygocactus in the greenhouse.

"*That's* a cactus?" I exclaimed when she came back carrying this strange-looking plant.

"It's for you," Roger said.

"Yeah? How come you're buying me a cactus?"

"You've been sick, haven't you?" he said gruffly, as if I shouldn't ask.

He motioned for me to pay, so I got out his money and spent most of it for this smooth-skinned plant creature that branched out like no cactus I'd ever seen.

On the way back to Sunnyside, I expected him to give me the lowdown on the Zygocactus, but he didn't. He just held it on his knees the way you would a baby and looked pleased with himself.

We found a nice sunny spot behind the nursing home, right next to the exit ramp. I parked Roger and set the wheelchair brake; I took the cactus off his lap, then plopped down next to it there on the curb.

"Someone's burning leaves," Roger concluded after sniffing the air.

"It's against the law now, did you know that?"

"What isn't?" he said, sucking on the empty pipe. "You know, Buddy, I keep thinking about those little pines. Half of them are going to die. More than half, likely."

"Why do you think that?"

"People won't plant 'em, won't take care of 'em. A tree needs a chance to grow up and be somebody."

"Yeah." I thought of the majestic tall masts of ships.

Roger tapped his pipe out on the metal frame of the wheelchair, as if that would improve the smell or the taste. He started talking again once it was back in his mouth. "The good book says there's a time to be born and a time to die."

"I've heard that."

"Then there are pages and pages telling a body how to live during those in-between years. . . . Wish I could smoke this durned thing!"

I laughed.

"But," he went on, "I can't think of a single line that tells a person how to go about dying. Buddy, I want you to listen—" His tone got very serious. "I've been around long enough. I'm ready to die."

My breath stopped. *First Henessey, now Roger!*

"Why are you saying that?" I cried.

"Because it's true. A man shouldn't be afraid of the truth."

"You're not going to die for years and years. Look at old Jacob!"

"Lord no! Ten more years would kill me," Roger mumbled.

Any other time I'd have cracked up over that.

"The thing is, Buddy, you're like one of those trembling new pines, all eager . . . full of it. The old guys, they've had a monopoly on the sun and rain in the forest. One day they have to make room for the shoots, the pretty little seedlings. It's nature's way. Keeps things going."

His voice was downright gruff when he said, "Tell you the truth, I'm tired. I'm tired of taking up space, and I'm no use to anybody, God knows, not even to me."

"Yeah, but you're not taking up any space of mine!" The words came out in a rush. "You just make my space better. All the time you do."

Roger smiled, looked off toward the mountains. "It's what I want, don't you see?"

"No," I answered. "I don't see, and I don't think you should talk like this."

So he didn't. He quit talking. I didn't say anything either. We just sat there being quiet, though my heart thumping inside my chest wasn't quiet at all.

When he spoke again, it was more like he was talking to himself. "I'd have said the same thing at your age. Dying isn't a very popular topic of conversation. Nobody wants to discuss it with you."

As his words soaked in, I began to feel funny. It came to me that Roger was the one who brought it up. *I* was the coward who couldn't stand to talk about dying, couldn't stand to think about it, even.

"Oh, I'll discuss dying with you," I hurried to say, "it's just that I don't . . . I mean . . ."

"No, no, it's all right, it's not your time, you shouldn't have to think about it. I just want you to know that when it happens—well—it's okay with me."

I chucked a pebble out onto the drive. I couldn't imagine what my life would be like without Roger. Didn't he feel the same way?

"You listening, Buddy?" I felt his pipe poking my shoulder. "This is your captain speaking, and by Neptune, you'd better be listening!"

"Yeah, I hear you." I picked up another rock and tossed it from hand to hand, but I couldn't look up at him.

"Your father, now, that was different. It's a real tragedy when a man dies young. A person cut down in his prime . . . like Lowell Max, losing his life at sea . . . all that crew, young men . . ."

I stared at my cactus sitting there on the sidewalk, soaking up the sun, and wished we were anywhere else talking about anything but dying. I thought of the forward deck house on the *Cutty Sark* and how much fun it would be to assemble. Roger would be around to see it all finished, I knew he would. It was Christmas making him sad, the way it made all the old folks sad.

Finally Roger told me he was getting chilled, so I stood up and pushed him back inside. When we reached the men's wing, he was too tired for anything but a nap.

"We'll work on that mizzenmast one of these days," he said, and I got the idea he felt bad about how the afternoon turned out.

"Keep your Zygocactus in the sun at home," he told me while I put away his coat and scarf. "Water it some. If you don't drown it, it'll surprise you come Christmas."

I pushed him close to the bed so he could ring for an aide then ended up trying to tease him into a better mood. "Will it sprout stickers like a regular cactus?" I asked.

He waved me away. "Go on, get outa here! Let an old walrus have some rest, why don't you?"

I started to leave, but I turned back when I heard him cussing and struggling with his dresser drawer. I put the pipe away for him, but maybe I shouldn't have. He hated it when he couldn't do things for himself.

"Now go, go," he said again, sawing the air with his hand. "You ought to be out playing with friends your age. There's no future throwing in with me."

"Aw, now you're sounding like my mom."

He grumbled some more, something I couldn't understand, then gave me another cross look.

"Okay, I'm leaving," I said and picked up my cactus.

"Your mother's right. This is no place. I'm too old to be worrying about you and me both."

"Me?" I whirled around. "You don't have to worry about me!"

"I'm not going to, not anymore."

I took my plant and went out into the hall.

"You've got it backward," I said under my breath. "I'm the one who has to worry about you all the time."

I zipped up my parka and left by the rear exit. I felt lots worse than when I came. Why would anybody want to die? Especially Roger. Expecially now when he was practically good as new again. None of it made any sense.

CHAPTER
·12·

Sprinting to school in the half-dark so Carmela and I wouldn't have to cross paths, I nearly ran a guy off the sidewalk.

"Hey, watch it!" he growled.

I swung around and nearly died. It was the soccer coach I'd clipped!

"What's the hurry, Palmer?"

I danced backward a few steps, breathing hard. "Sorry . . . didn't mean to get so close."

"How you doing?" he worked his arms and shoulders a little, broke into a jog. "Wait up, I could stand some exercise."

I cut down a driveway and waited for him on the street.

"You live around here?" he asked.

"Yeah." My breath came out in frosty puffs as I slowed to his pace, wishing to heck I'd left home earlier.

"Ran out of gas, had to park my Toyota." He grinned at me. "My own fault. I knew I was pushing it."

I didn't know what to say, so I just kept pumping along beside him.

He slid down the zipper of his jacket. "I've noticed you running to school before. You're a darn good sprinter, you know that? Ever think about track?"

"Nah, I only run when I have to get someplace fast."

We went on pounding the pavement together until the junior high loomed ahead of us. By that time I could tell the jogging was harder on him than it was on me, which made me feel pretty good. Also, I got the idea that Mr. Thurston wasn't as mad about the soccer business as I thought he was.

We crossed Seventeenth Street, then split up when he headed for the gym doors.

"See you, Palmer. You think about track now," he shouted before going inside. I flung a polite "See you" over my shoulder and took off around the building like a second-stage rocket.

I probably should have read my horoscope that morning. No doubt it said "Stay in bed, what's the use?" Carmela caught me at my locker, and—because I didn't see her first—we ended up face to face.

"I have to talk to you," she said in an icy voice.

I went on pulling out my English and science books. "About what?"

"About coming to Sunnyside. I wouldn't bother you if I didn't have to, but our scout troop wants to do a program when we hand out the bibs. Kim's mother, Mrs. Phillips, needs to know who to call."

"Her name's Mrs. Purdy. She's the social director."

"Thank you." Carmela turned on her heel and walked off without another word.

I followed her down the hall, tingling to think we were standing that close. Suddenly it occurred to me that I was being too hard on Carmela. There she was, sewing up bibs, practicing a program to entertain the folks at Sunnyside, and I was treating her like dirt. It could be she'd hate me forever.

That thought turned my tingles to megashivers in a hurry. Why was I acting so snotty to her? What happened to friendship, anyway? So she didn't show up when she said she would! Maybe she had an excuse. But why didn't she call me? Why didn't she find some way to tell me?

I hung around the dry cleaners after school, thinking I might be able to make things up between us, but Carmela never came along. Actually, I was relieved. I zipped on home, watered my Zygocactus, did some chores, then headed for Sunnyside.

I'd promised Mrs. Purdy I'd deliver Christmas cards to the rooms again, a job I liked a lot. Lucky Lucy once gave me five sticks of gum that fell out of a card from her great-grandchild. "Gum sticks to my choppers," she'd told me with a scrunched-up face, then made me chew them all at once.

While I visited with her that day, Lucy told me how she'd found a dollar's worth of loose change in the drawer of her nighstand. "Bought myself some salty potato chips at the machine and been piecin' the whole time. Ever see anyone so lucky?"

I acted totally amazed, but I knew who it was that planted money around for Lucy to find. (And it wasn't Smitty!)

With all the mail and the poinsettias and the music, Sunnyside at Christmas was more like a circus than a convalescent home. Carolers lined up in the halls like planes on a runway. The high-school *a cappella* group came, the Methodist bell-ringers, the *Godspell* troupe from the university, Santa's Cloggers.

As Roger said, chuckling, "They send the cello player to put us to sleep so the Salvation Army brass band can wake us up again."

There was so much Christmas cheer, you'd have thought the old-timers would OD on it. They didn't, though, because most of them couldn't remember what happened yesterday. When I asked Laura (between kisses) if she'd been to any good programs lately, she said, "Not for ages. Wish they'd get something goin' around here!"

I was the one who flipped out when Girl Scout Troop #253 appeared on the activity schedule. "Christmas Around the World," it said. We were in the hold working when I told Roger the good news. He'd just finished explaining why the standing rigging had to be black and the running rigging brown, and we'd stopped for a root beer.

"How come you haven't brought your girlfriend to Sunnyside lately? Is it because I'm such a grouch?" he asked.

"Heck no." I hesitated. "It's . . . well . . . Jim Needham

says if a girl doesn't pay any attention to him he just says 'Bag her.' So that's what I did."

"Bag her! Sounds rough. She's an awful pretty girl."

"Yeah. Nice, too."

He took a long swig from his can. After wiping off his mouth he said, "Maybe you ought to give her another chance."

"I been thinking about it."

"Did she treat you bad?"

"No, not exactly."

"Did she stab you in the back, kick you when you were down?"

"No."

His mustache twitched. "Well, then, she's not dangerous."

I grinned.

"Give her another chance, Buddy. Take it from someone who handed out enough second chances in his day to sink a lifeboat."

I told him I might, then Roger and I got back to work on the Sark. Funny how much better I always felt after talking things over with him.

The Friday before Christmas, I arrived at Sunnyside ahead of the Girl Scouts. For the first time since his stroke, Captain Ericksen was at the mike telling everyone where to go, and his voice sounded terrific.

"It's a 'Best,' " I pointed out to Natalie, who laughed and agreed.

She and I then divided up Main and West and started getting people to the activity room. I popped into Laura and Evaline's first and told them to get their walkers in gear. Then I took Carl and Glen and Donald. Finally, I got Zoe Becker and Schultz, who were married during the summer but couldn't stand to live together. At least they were holding hands during programs again.

They started out having private dinners in Zoe's room, their trays bright with flowers Natalie stole from the garden. "It's soooooo romantic," she'd said, "finding love in one's eighties." (Natalie had tried to give them a candlelight dinner one night, but Mom stopped her: "Natalie! They'll burn the place down.")

We were all disappointed when the flames of their love went out and they staged the worst mashed-potato fight ever witnessed at Sunnyside.

I found Roger on West, wearing his captain's hat and trying to pull his wheelchair along by the handrail mounted to the wall. One foot was helping out, but the other dragged like an anchor.

"Need a boost?" I asked.

"Guess so," he muttered, "if I want to see Carmelita."

We found a spot at the back of the activity room, and just in time. The Scouts were already filing in as a lady played Christmas songs on the piano. Half the girls were in uniform, the other half were wearing costumes and makeup. When I saw "Carmelita" in this big-skirted white dress with birds and flowers all over it, I knew I'd been a fool.

Roger poked me to point her out. As if he needed to. Her black hair was all done up with red flowers. She was wearing a lace scarf and tiny little heels, and she looked about sixteen. I nearly died of regret.

They started their program with "Feliz Navidad," singing the words in Spanish, which I figured Carmela had taught them. She played one set of maracas, Kim Phillips the other. The second time through we all clapped to the music. It didn't matter that the rhythm got ragged, because everyone was having fun.

Then the girls in costume took turns introducing themselves and the countries they were from. Ho Lan gave her own name because she really, truly is Vietnamese. I worried a little when I saw Carmela was going to be last. Activities were sometimes too long for the residents.

The program went on about forty minutes before Hanako got up to prance around with a Japanese fan. I couldn't figure out what her mincey little steps and the plinky music had to do with Christmas, but maybe Kim had the costume for a recital or something. Her dance took so long I could hear the snorers begin. I could also hear Evaline grumbling around.

My palms got sweaty because I knew The Cusser was building up to something worse. A minute later, sure enough, Evaline interrupted with a loud, "I'm tired of looking at you! Why don't you just sit down?"

The Girl Scouts looked horrified. Kim stopped dancing altogether.

After a little confusion, during which Mrs. Phillips kept nodding for the show to go on, Kim rushed through a few more bobs and dips then took her seat. I started breathing again, but I felt sorry for Kim and was sweating blood for Carmela, whose part was coming up.

Thank goodness Carmela's music was a loud mariachi tape. Everybody got back in the spirit as she twirled around in her bright dress. I relaxed, too, and started planning what I was going to say to her after the program.

When the music quit, she stepped to the mike and told us all about the custom of piñatas. Everyone went "Ooooh" when she held up a paper donkey painted every color of the rainbow.

"Today," she said, "instead of hitting the piñata with a stick, we want you to punch it with your fist." She gave the paper donkey a couple of easy pokes. "Like this, all right?"

Before I knew it, Carmela was marching straight up the aisle toward me. I was about to slide out of sight when I realized it was Roger she was after. He was grinning from ear to ear by the time she stopped in front of him.

"You be first, Señor Ericksen," she said.

Roger doubled up his fist and destroyed the donkey's left rib cage.

Everyone laughed. Gary shouted, "Way to go, Roger!" from the hallway, where he'd been watching.

The lady at the piano started in again with "Feliz Navidad" as Carmela moved along the rows, encouraging the residents to take a punch and help themselves to the candy inside. She didn't once look at me. I wouldn't have gotten a single candy if Roger hadn't shared his.

As it turned out, the Scouts were a big success. Especially when they distributed Christmas presents to every resident attending.

"Isn't this lovely?" Janice said to her neighbor, touching the bow and the tiny pine cones on her package. "The girls were just divine," she gushed a minute later to Mrs. Phillips. "I feel *so* uplifted!"

Roger hrrumphed.

I saw Natalie motioning me to start pushing wheel-chairs into the hall so the walkers could get through. The whole time, I'd been keeping an eye on Carmela, who was already helping Natalie ahead of me. Since I didn't want to be too obvious when I made my move, I decided to take Zoe Becker to her room first. When Ronald Schultz insisted on visiting his new wife, I had to take him there, too.

"We'd like room service for dinner tonight," Mr. Schultz told me before I left. "Please inform the cook." (I mean, like this is the Sheraton-Arms!)

Roger was gone when I returned to the activity room. So was Natalie. So was Carmela, matter of fact. The other Scouts were in the halls, pushing wheelchairs, trying to find people's rooms. That could take the rest of the day and the help of the entire staff.

When Carmela didn't come and *didn't* come, and the girls started drifting back in, I took off toward the west hall to find her.

She was in Roger's room, all right. She was standing by the ship's wheel and Roger was telling her all about it, pointing to this and that, explaining how a wheel that size could steer a mighty ship.

Their backs were to me, so I didn't see the bib at first. When Roger rolled to one side so Carmela could steer, I saw she'd already tied her pea-green bib on over his nice white shirt and tie. Captain Ericksen in a bib! I'd never seen anything so silly in my life. What really frosted me was that he didn't seem to care. He looked happy as a clam being with her.

I walked on down the hall to the hold. I turned on the work light and tried to remember just where it was we left off the last time.

I opened a jar of paint, winced as the sharp smell went zinging up my nose. I rolled a dry brush between my fingers until it collapsed, then pulled up a chair and sat down. I didn't want to think about anything else right then but being on the *Cutty Sark* and taking another tea run to China.

CHAPTER
·13·

Christmas came and went. The Zygocactus broke out with beautiful pink blooms all over it. Mom said she knew all along it was going to do that, but it sure was a surprise for me.

I took it to Sunnyside so Roger could enjoy it a few days. He loved it. He told me its common name was "Christmas cactus" and said it was the best present I could have given him. I bought him a box of chocolate-covered cherries, too, which he shared with everyone who stopped by.

Natalie and I were going to shop for a new vest for Roger, but things got so wild at the last minute we never did. Mostly because she started dating Gary, our bearded therapist with the incredible Schwarzenegger physique. Suddenly all Natalie could talk about was Gary and pumping iron, both boring subjects as far as I was concerned.

Troy was home only a week, but it was long enough for

my muscles to go on strike. Every day he had me up at seven for laps around the high-school track. It would still be dark, but here comes old Troy, bursting into the privacy of my room, yelling, "Roll out, you sleep hog!"

I'd hang onto the covers for dear life, but it wouldn't do any good.

"You'll thank me for this someday," he'd shout gleefully as he dumped me out on the floor.

What could I do? I was no match. Somehow I'd haul on my sweats and stumble out of the house alongside my brother, Rambo.

Mom called us "the odd couple." Anyone seeing us run together would know why. Here's old Troy, threatening to split out of his polypropylene shirt. Beside him on the track, an incredibly good sport, comes Tom Palmer, huffing along in his oversize Hastings College sweats. Next to the ultimate jock, I looked like a candidate for the fat farm.

I was actually starting to enjoy those workouts a little when I realized it was Troy's last morning at home. We were at the bleachers, bent over and tying our shoes when I thought about it. With his cheeks red from the cold and his hair falling forward, Troy looked about as All-American as you can get. To think I'd have to go through missing him all over again!

I was embarrassed to be caught staring, but Troy just grinned. "Feel that leg," he invited.

All warm, brotherly thoughts took off. "Not bad," I observed, poking my own cushy thigh.

"Not yours, dummy! Mine. Go ahead, see how hard it is."

Dutifully I squeezed his twenty-four-inch thigh. "Wow, Troy! Reinforced steel!"

He yanked up his socks, straightened to tower over me. "Legs don't get that way overnight, you know."

"No kidding!" (As if I hadn't already noticed his thick neck and bulging biceps and magnificent quadriceps.)

About then, wired to the max for our last workout, Troy began hopping around and smacking me on the arm. What was a mere tap for him knocked me clean over. He laughed, but he helped me up and surprised me with a bear hug that nearly finished me off.

"Hey, Tom, you little poop, you're coming along without me . . . shot up a foot since September. Your speed's good, stamina's great. Really great for a kid your age."

When he finally turned me loose and we got on the track, I ran better than even I thought possible.

Afterward, walking along toward McDonald's, I worked up enough nerve to ask Troy a question.

"Something's been bothering me," I began. "I almost wrote you about it."

"Okay, so shoot. I'm listening."

I told him how I'd argued with Jim Needham and the rest of the class in English that day and how I thought most of those guys were wrong. I explained about the story we'd read and about mercy killing and living wills and all that. He listened, nodding as we walked.

"So what's the question?"

"Do you think someone like . . . well, say, Dad . . . Do you think he'd have wanted a pill or a shot when he had leukemia? To end it all, I mean?"

Troy studied the ground. He took a long time thinking it

over, but when he looked up he said, "Maybe. At the end. The pain was really bad before he died." He gave me a bump with his elbow. "Why's it bugging you so much?"

"You think it's right? Could *you* . . . I mean, isn't it wrong to, you know, just take your own life or . . . or kill someone else?"

He frowned. "If I was the guy with the cancer and I positively knew I couldn't live . . . I don't think I'd see it as killing."

I didn't have a chance to say anything more because he hooked me around the neck and lifted me off my feet. "You think too much, Tom. That's your whole problem."

"Yeah," I gagged, hoping he'd leave me something to think *with*.

By then we'd arrived at McDonald's, where we were going to have breakfast and spend the gift certificates Mom gave us for Christmas. I hadn't got much of an answer out of Troy, but I knew I'd think about what he'd said for days. Sometimes I wished I could be more like him. It would be easier. "Get physical" was his solution for everything.

We went on in and ordered a couple of giant breakfasts. I was about to ask for milk to go with mine when Troy jumped in with "Add another coffee to that, please."

I pulled back. "I never drink coffee."

He knuckled me in the ribs. "You'll be shaving off that peach fuzz one of these days. A cup of coffee won't hurt you."

I was planning to tell Troy about Carmela once we lit into breakfast, but I changed my mind. It was just as well. Troy was so wound up I couldn't have got a word in. He went on and on. About his games, life in the dorm, about how college made junior high look like preschool. Even about their gaggy cafeteria food.

"I don't get anything this good," he said, devouring a potato patty in two bites.

"So—Tom," he said when he got tired of talking about himself, "are the girls leaving you alone these days?"

I grinned, shrugged.

"No girlfriends, huh?"

I shrugged again.

"Aw, come on."

I stirred a second pack of sugar into my coffee so I could stand to drink it. "Carmela, maybe. I'm not sure."

He shook his head and laughed. "I thought so. Mom told me what your teacher said."

I sat up straight. "What do you mean?"

"At the parent-teachers conference. About you discovering girls. Don't get me wrong, girls are great! But you have to keep them in perspective, you know what I mean? You have to study, make some grades so you'll get somewhere in this world."

I gave him a slit-eyed look. "Is this a father-son talk we're having or what?"

He threw his head back and laughed. "Yeah, so pay attention!"

I started on my second Egg McMuffin, wondering how it would be if it really *was* my dad sitting there across the table from me. He probably wouldn't be fidgeting with a stir stick the way Troy was, getting ready to bend and spring it at me.

In a minute Troy said, "I guess I never told you, but I

promised Dad I'd—you know—look after you while you were growing up. So you wouldn't turn into some kinda nerd."

"Nerd!" I snorted into my cup of juice. "Since when do I need someone looking after me?"

"You don't. You're doing okay. It's Mom who gets nervous sometimes. Thinks you need a role model." He started to chuckle. "Remember when you were little and she found you shaving your legs with a play razor? That was so funny but she about died."

I'd heard the story too many times.

"Anyway," he said, "I just want you to know you can go ahead and write to me when you feel like it. You know, if you ever want to ask something about Dad. Or Carmela . . . or anything."

I nodded.

"Or call me. Someday you may just want to pick up the phone and . . . well, shoot the bull with me or something. So call. Mom won't care."

The smile he gave me was ten times more warming than the coffee.

A minute later he destroyed the great moment when he leaned over and whispered, "You little nerd!"

I gave him a kick under the table. That was followed by getting my knees crushed between his. So much for sibling harmony!

My biggest disappointment was that I couldn't get Troy to Sunnyside even once to see the *Cutty Sark*, which was finally shaping up to look like a seagoing vessel. He ran out of time. As it was, he only saw a few football buddies and one old girlfriend before he had to leave.

"I'll see it when it's finished," he promised as he packed the cotton shirts Mom had been ironing all morning. His next vacation was spring break, and that seemed eons away.

At the airport we waited an hour and forty minutes, were nervous wrecks before Troy's 727 taxied in. When at last they called for seating between rows five and fifteen, Mom got out her Kleenex and my throat went dry.

"Listen, kid," Troy said when it was time for parting words. "I want you to keep on training. You could do something in track if you put your mind to it."

"Tell me about it!" I smarted back. What I really felt like was crying.

He told me about it all right. His answer was a blow to the shoulder that might have killed me. Fortunately I ducked, leaped away, and tore off down the B Concourse, thereby saving my own life. When I came back, Mom was wiping her eyes and Troy was gone.

CHAPTER
·14·

With Troy gone and school starting again, things promised to settle back to normal, the way they always do after Christmas vacation. There had been so much excitement through the holidays, I hated the thought of an ordinary January. "Back to the real world!" was the way Mom put it.

As it turned out, Carmela waited for me on her porch that first morning, the same as she'd done before Thanksgiving. For some reason, I almost expected her to. Maybe not seeing each other for ten days had cleared the air for us to begin again. Or maybe having fun with Troy made me forget how much she'd disappointed me.

"Hello, Tom," she called as she bounced down the steps.

I was the first to smile. "Hi, Carmela!" (Thank goodness she smiled back.)

"How was Christmas?" she asked.

"Great. Troy was home." I didn't tell her he ran me

ragged or that there were now two pounds less of me than before.

"We were at my cousins' in Denver for a week. It was so neat."

"Yeah?" I glanced at her profile and my feet suddenly turned clumsy, like I needed to plot every step.

"Is Roger wearing his bib?"

"Every chance he gets." (The laundry loses everything else, you'd think they could lose that pea-green bib.)

"Are you over being mad at me?" Carmela asked right out.

I looked ahead. "How come you didn't come over to Sunnyside that day?"

"Why didn't you give me a chance to explain why I didn't?"

We moved to one side to accommodate a jogger coming up behind us.

"Hey, Palmer!" the guy said, and I realized it was Coach Thurston.

"Did you run out of gas again?" I yelled.

"Just jogging . . . New Year's resolution . . . You signing up for track?" he hollered back over his shoulder.

"Not hardly!"

I'd had my fill of exercise for awhile, but I was impressed that he'd be running on such a cold morning.

Carmela merely looked puzzled by the whole business. "So—," she persisted, "don't you want to know why I didn't get to the Thanksgiving party?"

"Yeah, sure—tell me."

"Mrs. Phillips—you know, Kim's mom, who's our troop leader?—she called me that day as soon as I got home. She works, you know, and she said that was the only time she could take me to the fabric store. I'd planned the whole bib-making project, so I had to go with her."

My feeble "oh" hung on the frosty air.

"When I called you later that night, your Mom said she'd put you to bed with the flu."

"You talked to her—," I squeaked, "and she never told me?"

"I made you a Get Well card, too, but I got mad and threw it away."

I wanted to tell her I was sorry.

"I saw Roger Sunday," she said, bubbling on about how she took him and Janice some peanut butter cookies she'd made. "I told him you weren't speaking to me any more. Anyway, he said life's too short to hold grudges. He said I should make up with you if you didn't have the gumption to make up with me."

"He said that?" I squeaked again, knowing good and well he did.

Carmela made with a little skip, so I knew our conversation wasn't half as hard on her as it was on me.

She gave me an impish look. "Guess what else?"

I was afraid to.

"I took a volunteer's application home from Sunnyside. Mama said I could be an after-school volunteer if it didn't interfere with homework. Natalie said the aides could use my help any time I wanted to come in."

I swallowed a mouthful of saliva. I was glad at first, then I wasn't.

Carmela laughed. "Do you think I'll make a good volunteer? I have a lot to learn, of course. I don't know the people the way you do, and I still don't think I could let Laura kiss me—"

She rattled on, mentioning how nice Agnes was at the program and telling me how much she liked Mrs. Purdy, who interviewed her. Then she got back to Roger and the funny conversation they'd had Sunday when he'd tried to practice his Spanish on her.

I felt a little twinge. She was having all the fun while Mom and I were waiting around the airport with Troy. It made me sorry all over again that Troy didn't get to Sunnyside. My brother and my best friend: They hardly knew each other.

"I can't go today, though," Carmela broke in. "They have to approve my application at a staff meeting. Anyway, I have a baby-sitting job this week. Mrs. Filipowski is bringing her twins to our house after school."

I was relieved to know she was busy. It would take some getting used to, having Carmela at Sunnyside. Well it was my own fault. *I* was the one who dragged her over there, but I never dreamed she'd want to volunteer. When you have a close friend like Roger—almost a relative, for heck's sake—you're not exactly thrilled to have someone else butting in. After all, Captain Ericksen and I had been through a lot together. He was my friend a long time before he was hers.

Roger was pretty excited when I got to Sunnyside after school. He was sitting in the doorway of his room, waiting for me and ready to roll.

"We got to check something on that ship," he said, "some markings I think they left off."

I got behind him to hurry things up.

Once in the hold, I threw down my notebook and switched on the light. He spread out the assembly instructions, flipped pages, looked through the stick-ons. "You can't trust 'em," he growled. "There's nothing here at all."

"What's missing?"

"Give me some paper. I'll have to draw a picture of it."*

I ripped a sheet out of my notebook, gave him the pencil I kept in my hip pocket. I leaned over his shoulder and watched him draw a circle the size of a dime. It was shaky, but it was a circle. Then he put a line straight across and through it, with an *L* on one side and an *R* on the other.

"That's for left and right, I'll bet."

"No, it's not." He continued adding letters, *FW* to the right and just above the circle, an *S* to the left and just below the circle.

He sat back, then, and handed me the paper. "This is called a Plimsoll Mark. It was invented by an Englishman named Plimsoll for safety at sea. Has to do with what loads a ship can carry in different waters." He paused to let the words soak in.

"It was used by all cargo-carrying ships such as the full-rigged *Cutty Sark*, still *is* used today." He leaned forward and pulled the hull of the *Sark* toward us.

"Right there," he pointed, "smack dab between fore and aft, and—oh—about this far down." He showed me. "You paint it on in white with a nice, fine line."

"What do those letters mean?"

——————————— This is deck line of ship

FW.

.L ⊕ R.

FW = Fresh Water
L = Lloyds
R = Register

S.

S = Salt Water North Atlantic Ocean
— = line in Disk = load in any water
at summer

The "Plimsoll mark" found on the side of cargo-carrying ships such as the full-rigged Cutty Sark was invented by Englishman Samuel Plimsoll. In 1876, Parliament passed the Merchant Shipping Act, which required this mark on all ocean-going British ships; it indicates the maximum weight to which a ship can be safely loaded. The center line through the disk must not be submerged at any time in salt water. "FW" indicates the line to which a ship may load in fresh water, and "SW" indicates the line to which she may load in salt water in the winter North Atlantic Ocean. The practice of using this mark began to be applied to foreign ships leaving British ports, and eventually spread to other nations.

"The L and R stand for Lloyd's Registry. It's like a . . . well, a certificate from the British government."

"Because the *Cutty Sark*'s British, huh?"

"The *FW* and S stand for fresh water and salt water. She can load to the FW mark in fresh water, or to the S in salt water. The lines show the depths a ship will sink to when properly loaded. It's different for different waters, you see?"

I wasn't sure I understood, but I nodded.

Roger took great pains to print "Plimsoll Mark" at the top of the notebook paper. "If I had time, Buddy, I'd write those kit people a sharp letter. What good's a model if it isn't authentic?"

"Well, this one's going to be authentic!" I wanted to tell him how lucky I was to have an honest-to-goodness ship's captain on board, but I was too embarrassed to say it.

Roger decided that painting the figurehead would be a good job for him, so that's what he did next. There was no detail, so it didn't matter if he slopped the white paint a little. While he was doing that, I got another coat of antiquing on the forward deck house we'd assembled.

"Know what the name of this clipper ship means?" he said as we worked.

"Was she named after the whiskey?"

Roger chuckled. "The other way around. The whiskey was named after the ship." He held up the figurehead, which was a lady with long flowing hair and one arm outstretched. "The words 'cutty sark' mean a kind of skimpy dress, like what she's wearing here."

"You're kidding me!" I straightened. "This ship's named after a shortie nightgown?"

Roger's mustache twitched. "That's about it."

"Oh my heck!"

He dipped in the jar of white and started painting her tiny curved hand.

"I wouldn't mind taking charge of this schooner," he talked on. "With such nice, slim lines she could slip through the water like an eel. She set some speed records in her time, running tea and Australian wool both."

"Wish we were shipping out to Australia right now," I said. "Wouldn't that be radical? See all those kangaroos."

"All those *sheep*," he muttered, wiping off his brush. "Oh, I suppose I could set sail in the morning if I had to, how about you?"

"I got three bags packed already."

Roger smiled. "You know what they say, Buddy. The more experienced the sailor, the less gear he carries around."

Roger set the figurehead on the table to dry. He cleaned his hands with the paint rag, then settled back in the wheelchair. "Of course that may not be true nowadays. About the gear." He took out his pipe. "In my day—oh hell, Buddy, I've got to quit talking about my days. An old man gets out of touch."

I reached for the rag. "You're not so old."

"Monstrous old."

He made a funny sucking noise with his pipe that caused us to grin at each other.

I stood back, then, to admire Roger's paint job and my

antiquing, and pointed out that a captain is supposed to be older and smarter than his first mate. It wouldn't be right if he wasn't. Roger nodded. He agreed.

I left Sunnyside feeling really happy. Roger said we'd finish the Sark by tuliptime if we didn't slack off.

Eating the two man-size burritos Mom left in the fridge, I even got a little excited about Carmela's news. Things would work out, I guessed, if she didn't start hanging around the hold with us.

I was feeling so good, in fact, I started rehearsing the phone call I planned to make after eight o'clock, the time Mrs. Filipowski was scheduled to pick up her twins.

"Carmela," I planned to say, "could you refresh my memory about Jean Henessey's assignment in English?" (We liked using our teachers' first names behind their backs.)

An hour later when Mom came home from work, I forgot all about Carmela.

"Roger had a heart attack," she said before she even took off her coat.

CHAPTER
·15·

I jumped up from the sofa where I'd been watching TV. "Heart attack! Mom, is he—"

"He's hanging on. Dr. Grogan's already seen him, but it sounds—" she shook her head. "It's not good."

I grabbed up my coat, but Mom hauled it away from me before I could get one arm in the sleeve.

"No way, Tom! He's critical."

"But, Mom," I yelled at her, "they don't always pay attention over there! What if Roger calls and they ignore him? You know yourself—"

She grabbed me by the shoulders. "Listen to me. Smitty got a special-duty nurse for him tonight. That's why I'm late, because I sat with him until she came. Now just calm down."

"Okay, okay, I'm calm!" I pulled away, furious to have our perfect day end in such a heap. I'd scarcely recovered from Roger's stroke and now it was something else. Who could be calm?

"What happened to him?" I asked, following Mom to the kitchen where she put a cup of water in the microwave.

"He complained of chest pains in the dining room, collapsed in the hall. Wheeling himself back to the room, I guess. He's medicated and on oxygen, but they're worried." She shook her head. "He's had a number of these, Tom. You have to prepare yourself. Things look worse this time."

She threw her coat on a chair, then took the hot chocolate out of the cupboard for me. I shook my head no. She made herself a cup of coffee, then slid dejectedly into a chair at the table and kicked off her shoes.

Looking up, she said, "Mrs. Purdy was trying to reach Roger's daughter in Phoenix."

"Will she come?"

"She didn't last time. Who knows?"

I stuck my cold hands in my armpits, then glanced up to see Mom's profile reflected in the dark window glass. She looked as beat as I'd ever seen her.

"Tom"—she reached out and pulled me into her side—"Roger lived a long, full life. He isn't afraid. He's told me that himself. Sometimes the greatest bravery is just—accepting. Accepting what has to be. Do you know that?"

I didn't answer, but I wondered if she was thinking about Dad when she said "accepting." Maybe she was thinking about herself, too.

A minute later I went after the paper and brought it in to her.

"Thanks," she smiled. "You're a good kid. How did you know I was too tired to move?"

"I could tell."

I'm the one who has to keep moving. Suddenly I was cold all the way to the bone marrow.

I went upstairs to my room where I could be alone. I usually never pray, but that night I prayed. Maybe Roger wasn't afraid, but I was. I squeezed my hands together and begged God to let Roger live. I promised everything I could think of in return for that one little favor.

When I opened my eyes, I found myself wishing I had more pull with God. I sent a frantic glance around the room. What could I exchange for a favor? I didn't have much—the fern and cactus Roger gave me, clothes strung all over and hanging on my desk chair, my catalogs and models . . . a closetful of games . . .

Suddenly it struck me how silly I must sound. God didn't want my stupid stuff! I could have offered to trade myself—a life for a life—but I was too scared to do that. I was too big a coward. Besides, I reasoned, things just don't work that way.

I fell back across the bed. *You can't make deals, Tom Palmer. You can't pretend it's not going to happen, either. You have to be brave. Like Troy. He was only ten when Dad died.*

Talking tough didn't help much once the reruns began. I flashed on our times in the greenhouse, our two years' worth of fun in the hold, picnics in the courtyard with Natalie and Lucy and Janice. I thought of all Roger taught me about plants, about commercial shipping, life at sea. Even about how a person gets to age eighty-seven in the first place, for crying out loud!

I finally went back downstairs to watch TV, but I

couldn't concentrate. Mom's favorite police show that she never misses seemed whole precincts away from real life.

I went back up to my room, put on my pajamas. I knew I wouldn't sleep, but I stretched out anyway and stared at the bottoms of my boats. I tossed and turned, drew up my knees, threshed around until my blankets were all pulled out. It got to be ten-thirty.

Pretty soon Mom came in. "Roger wouldn't want you getting sick over him," she said. She sat on the edge of the bed and smoothed my hair. "Remember how worried and upset he was when you had the flu? He asked about you every day."

"He did?" I sat up. "He asked about me? How come you never tell me anything?" I gave her a hard stare. "Roger worries and you don't tell me. Carmela *calls*—you never tell me." I threw myself back onto the pillow. "Mom, when Troy gets a message you leave notes all over the house!"

She smiled as she pulled up my blankets. "I'm sorry, I forget a lot."

"Yeah," I said, kicking them off again. "A lot of good 'sorry' does!"

She stood up to leave.

"Don't go yet."

"I don't think you want me here."

"Well, okay—go. It just makes me mad, that's all."

She came back, felt for my foot and squeezed it. "I'll call Sunnyside first thing tomorrow. Now, you get some rest, you hear? There's nothing we can do tonight." In the dark her kiss landed on my eye.

When I finally did fall asleep, I dreamed Roger and I were on the *Cutty Sark* and there were sheep all over the deck, so many we didn't know what to do with them. They kept popping up out of the hold, making these sad, bleating sounds. Roger and I were screaming at each other across the sea of sheep, but we couldn't hear over their terrible noise. We were supposed to be loading bales of wool, not sheep.

I started heaving them over the side, one after another, but they never hit the water because it changed into a grassy meadow and they all ran away. Roger started helping me and we began to laugh. We laughed like a couple of crazy men, tossing all those sheep. Then Roger picked me up and threw me over the side . . .

I woke up breathing hard and fast, and I knew plain as day why I was scared. Roger was dying! It was really happening. I'd lost my father. My brother, too, in a way. I didn't think I could stand losing Roger.

I closed my eyes against the pitch black of my room and felt really, really alone.

CHAPTER
·16·

I wanted to go to Sunnyside before breakfast the next morning, but Mom said, "Absolutely not!" Since it had already started to snow and she had to buy groceries, anyway, she offered to drive Carmela and me to school.

I called Carmela and we picked her up on the way. I told her about Roger as soon as she got in the car.

"Oh, Tom, no!" she said, her forehead bunching up. Quickly she turned away. I stared at the snow blowing into the windshield and knew how she felt, how worried and helpless. She was never that quiet.

When we were almost to school, she asked if she could go visit him.

"Not yet," Mom answered. "His condition's the same this morning. I've asked Tom to wait, too."

No way! I said to myself. An armed SWAT team couldn't keep me away from Sunnyside.

It was about fifteen minutes into gym class and jump shot practice when I heard my name called.

"Mr. Thurston wants to see you in his office," my regular gym teacher hollered across the floor.

"Me? He wants to see *me*?"

"You're the only Tom Palmer around here. Run on down there now before we get a game started."

I dropped out of line and trotted off. Needham dribbled a ball across to where I was mopping my face with a towel. "What *didn't* you do this time, sucker?"

My hand snaked out and snapped the elastic on his gym shorts. I didn't have any more clue than he did.

I wasn't exactly scared when I walked into the other gym office, but I noticed a change in my breathing as soon as I closed the door behind me.

"Sit down, Palmer," Thurston said, so I did. (On the front edge of the chair.)

"I won't keep you out of class too long."

"Oh, that's okay," I said with a grin.

He shifted his weight a little, swiveled, and leaned back. He gave me a long look before saying, "Spring's just around the corner according to my calendar."

I figured he was rushing the season, but I flashed on my tulips when he said "spring." Then I saw Roger and suddenly remembered everything. How could there be a spring without Roger? It was his favorite season.

"What would it take to get you serious about track?" Thurston asked.

My mind snapped back like the elastic in Needham's shorts. "I don't know anything about track," I said, and it was the flat truth.

Mr. Thurston leaned forward on his elbows. "I guess you thought I was pretty hard on you that day in gym class."

I didn't know what to say, so I kept my eyes on the brass trophy that sort of loomed between us.

"Well, I was tough on you. I figured you needed it."

"Yessir."

"I didn't know who you were then, but I don't think it would have made any difference if I had."

I looked up, not sure what he meant.

"I kept track of your brother Troy all the way through high school," he went on. "Read about him in the sports section, saw him play a few games, including that tournament playoff. Remember? Where he busted through for an eighty-yard gain? Oh man!" He smacked the table with his hand and laughed, which made me laugh. "Now that was a game!"

"No kidding, you followed Troy's football?"

"I sure did. He was very solid. Obvious college material, even as a junior. It didn't surprise me at all when he got that scholarship. But—and I'm sorry about this, but it's true—" He made an embarrassed face. "I'd forgotten he had a little brother."

"Well—," I laughed nervously. "Me and Troy—we're not exactly alike, you know. I never played sports the way he does."

There was a long pause during which Mr. Thurston memorized my face. Finally he said, "It's my opinion that you've got more athletic ability than you think."

Wrong! I wanted to say.

"There are a lot of guys just like you in junior high. There's a kind of dormancy going on, you know what I mean? Suddenly one day all that clumsiness and lassitude turns into energy, and Pow! All a kid needs when that happens is a little bit of direction."

I couldn't control the doubtful look I felt creeping across my face.

"You couldn't be Jim Palmer's son and not be pretty well equipped for athletics," Thurston said as he shook his head. "And take my word for it, you're the spitting image of your dad."

"I am? I mean—you knew my dad, too?"

"Well, yes, in a way. Our schools were rivals. I saw more film footage of Jim Palmer in high school than of almost anyone."

"Yeah?" I found myself leaning forward.

"He was a hot quarterback in high school. We faced off in three different games. He was at South, I was at Skyline. Neither one of our teams made it through the playoffs the year we graduated, but we both came darned close."

Suddenly I was smiling like crazy. What a coincidence, Mr. Thurston knowing my dad! I could hardly believe it.

"Watching you heat up the sidewalks between your house and school has been like seeing Jim run all over again. Something about your stride . . . the chin up, the chest leading the way—" We ended up laughing and I could feel my heart beating in my ears. No one ever said I was like my dad before.

Then the office got quiet again. I thought maybe it was time for me to leave except that Mr. Thurston seemed to be thinking. He fingered a pen, put it down again.

"When your father died," he said, checking my face, "the Quarterback Club was represented at his funeral by a group of us who had played ball during his time. That's when we set up the scholarship fund, with every hope that Jim's son, who was still younger than junior high, would qualify for it some day. And Troy did. Has your mother told you all about that?"

I shrugged. I knew Troy had a Quarterback Club Scholarship, but that was all.

"Jim Palmer was a fine athlete, but I'm not saying a son has to take after his father in every respect. Some people just aren't cut out for team sports. They do better in the individual areas. But trust me, Tom, there's a first-class track man inside you. He's just waiting to get out. I'd like to be the one who helps develop that runner."

I felt lightheaded and happy. Suddenly Coach Thurston looked more like a friend than an enemy. *Felt* more like a friend, too, when he came around the desk and pumped my hand.

"Come and see me if you decide you'd like some coaching. In three, four years, unless I miss my guess, you'll be setting records your dad—or anyone—would be proud of."

I could feel my ears turning red.

He walked with me to the door of the office.

"Troy thinks I'm too fat," I blurted out, not knowing what else to say.

The coach squeezed the back of my neck. "You're losing it, kid, that's pretty obvious."

I sailed through the rest of the day, hoarding his words like a state secret. I wanted to tell Mom . . . and Carmela . . . and Roger and Natalie. I wanted everyone to know, but at the same time I didn't. I wanted something just for me, something special to think about.

I kept his words in my mind right up to the last bell of the day.

At 2:40 I was out of school and sprinting. Across Seventeenth, past the cleaners, the street where Carmela and I lived, McDonald's, the convenience store, the greenhouse. I heard the music from *Chariots of Fire* in my head, and my feet hardly touched the ground.

I was out of breath when I passed the redwood sign, but by the time I arrived at the big double doors of Sunnyside, I was thinking more about Roger than anything else. And I was scared. I said another quick "Please, God" at the door and went in.

I hurried along Main toward West, my heart pounding so hard I could hear it. People were still napping. Elaine's "da-da-da" sounded tired, as if she were dropping off. Around the corner I passed Carl, who slept in his doorway, curled over like the C of his name. Someone had forgotten to put him down.

My eyes stung when I saw the red stop sign on Roger's door. *He's alive, he's still going! Good old oxygen sign!*

I tiptoed into his room and across to the high, narrow bed. He was lying very still. When his eyelids fluttered, I whispered, "Roger?"

He didn't seem to hear me. "It's me, Tom . . . *Buddy!*" I corrected myself. "I been really worried about you."

No movement. He was in such a deep sleep he didn't know I was there.

I gripped the chrome railing and hung on until my breathing returned to normal.

I saw his shoulder twitch. The hand with the IV attached lifted slightly on the sheet, dropped again. I thought about how strong he was before the stroke and how he could make me wince any time we had a contest.

"Handling the ropes does it," he'd said many times. "A man develops strength where he needs it."

I studied his hand as it was now, fish-white and bulgy with veins. When I touched his fingers and nothing happened, I knew for sure he was somewhere else and not in his body.

I thought of my dream and all those sheep. Maybe Roger was on the *Cutty Sark* and was on his way to get some of that Australian wool. Seventy-two days around the Cape. I hoped there wouldn't be any storms.

When I left his bedside, it was to take command at the ship's wheel.

I looked out the window at the dirty snow bordering the parking lot, then let my imagination transform asphalt-and-all into a crystal South Pacific sea. The knobs felt solid and smooth under my hands. I executed a full right, and the gliding action of the wheel made me shiver.

"Buddy Palmer, what are you doing in here?"

I whirled around. It was Smitty.

"I'm . . . I came in to see Roger," I stammered, shoving my guilty hands into my back pockets.

"He's too ill for visitors. You go on out."

"Is he any better?" I dared to ask at the door, though she looked cross enough to put *me* on probation.

"I wish I could say he is. Stay out now, Buddy. You can't do him any good hanging around his room."

I could see why the aides hated Smitty. She was about as nice as a staph infection.

I started toward the kitchen to check in with Mom, then did an about-face when I realized I'd had orders not to come to Sunnyside at all. I doubled back. Maybe I'd just go sit in the hold for a while. If finishing the *Sark* was going to be up to me . . . I shuddered thinking about it. It was too complicated. There were too many things I didn't know about ships.

I turned on the work light and pulled up my chair. I opened the assembly manual to the drawings of the masts and rigging. If I could just get one mast seated, so she'd look more like a ship, so Roger, seeing it, would be encouraged . . .

I found the section detailing mast assembly. I took a deep breath and forced myself to concentrate.

"First," I read, "lash the heel of the jib-boom to the bowsprit, using the small diameter black thread."

Okay. So far, so good. I can do that.

I looked around for the jib-boom. *Where's the jib-boom?* I lifted the assembly instructions, sorted through the pieces laid out on the table. It had to be there. I felt around under the box that everything came in.

I straightened up to adjust the light when I noticed the root beer can Roger left on the table before Christmas. I don't know what happened, but it was like a cannon went off inside me.

I set that root beer can on the floor, then pounded it to death, my leg going up and down, up and down like a machine. Scooping up the can, I threw it against the wall with all my might.

And then my chest exploded. I fell back in the chair and covered my face with my hands. I was glad nobody was around to see me because I cried like a baby.

For the first time in my life, I really missed my father.

CHAPTER ·17·

By the time I got to Sunnyside after school the next day, Roger's daughter had come in on a plane from Phoenix. Though I'd seen her before, she wasn't the kind of person who'd remember me.

Mrs. Helen Marti was a big, tall woman, someone who looked as if she could command a whole fleet of ships without any help. She wore black slacks and had a way of sniffling between sentences that drove Natalie crazy.

Roger was now in a coma, according to Mom. I was glad I'd sneaked in to see him early—before school. With his daughter in the room nonstop, I'd never get a chance. My plan that day was to stick around after school and brush up on my volunteering skills. Sooner or later, I reasoned, Mrs. Marti would have to go to the dining room to eat.

When Mrs. Purdy asked me to take the activity calendars around to the residents' rooms and tape them up, I said I would. It was a job I would let Carmela do in the future because it wasn't one of my favorites. I began on

East, planning to work my way around the building clockwise to give myself some variety, but saving Lucky Lucy and Agnes for last. I needed to talk to Lucy. I hadn't told her about Roger yet.

I was nearly finished when I saw Gary and Natalie disappear through the "Employees Only" door to the basement.

I went into Donald's room and Scotty's, then into old Jacob's, where I had to find his glasses. He was working on another petition to end nuclear war. "He'll die trying" was what Roger said about him last week.

Although I wasn't planning to, I stopped at Roger's room when I noticed that Dr. Grogan was in there talking with Mrs. Marti. I knew they wouldn't chase me out when I was doing Sunnyside business, so I took my time removing the December calendar and taping the new one to the back of the door.

I heard the doctor say "congestive heart failure" and "very poor pulse" and I wished I knew what "congestive" meant. I couldn't see behind my back, but I knew Dr. Grogan was shaking his head by the sound of his voice.

Mrs. Marti spoke next. "Well, as I said before, my brother and I have agreed . . . and my father arranged everything ahead of time . . ." She sounded nicer than I remembered her. Kinder, not so bossy. "But it's enormously difficult . . . Doctor, I wish Gaylen were here!"

I stood there listening, even though I was finished, until I heard her heels on the floor. She crossed the room, lifted the schedule off the door, handed it back. "He doesn't need this. Put it in someone else's room."

I looked past her at Roger and guessed that nothing had changed since morning. Then I left.

The tone of the doctor's voice worried me and I wondered again what "congestive" meant. Was Dr. Grogan giving up? Wouldn't he keep trying, right up to the end?

Carrying my last few schedules, I decided to go downstairs to the aides' room to see if Natalie was there or in the laundry room digging for someone's clothes. Maybe she knew something more about Roger.

She was in the lounge, all right, sitting on the sofa with Gary, who was drinking a cup of coffee. They were holding hands, something they quit doing as soon as I walked in. I made a few gagging sounds, pretending to choke on the bad air in the room.

"Awful, isn't it?" Natalie grumbled.

I fanned my face. "How can you stand to breathe this stuff?" The smoke hanging in the room was ten times worse than Roger's pipe. "Does Smitty ever come in here?"

"It's our break room," Gary said, although I wasn't talking to him. "Where else would we go?"

"Buddy"—Natalie patted the sofa beside her—"how are you taking all this?"

I sat down. I rolled up the schedules and stared through the tube at the floor. I knew she meant Roger, but I didn't want to say anything in front of Gary.

"He was talking a little this morning," she told me.

I sprang forward. "He was?"

"He said a few words to his daughter, but then . . . This must be so hard for you."

"Yeah, Mrs. Marti's in there the whole time. What did he say?"

Natalie shook her head. "I don't know. Nothing coherent, I guess, but she thought he recognized her."

Gary looked at his watch, got up to leave.

"I'm taking five more," Natalie told him. "They can fire me if they don't like it." She hunched a shoulder at me and smiled her tough smile. I was glad when Gary, the Iron Man, went on back to work.

"I hate it because I can't see Roger," I said in a rush.

"I know."

"What does 'congestive' mean? Is it like having congestion, like when you get a cold?"

She studied her hands in her lap. "That's why I'm going to nurses' training next fall, to learn what some of these things mean. I feel terrible about Roger, too. I knew you'd be worried sick.

"Buddy—," she paused, as if thinking about her words. "I want to tell you something. I think you're old enough to know and I don't think anyone else is going to tell you."

She sounded so serious I held my breath. She turned to face me, taking my knees in her hands as if to keep me from running away.

"Roger signed a living will way back in the spring."

He did? A living will?

"Do you know what that is?"

I bit the inside of my cheek, but I didn't answer.

She went on. "It's a legal document a person signs, so that if you're really sick, terminally sick"—she frowned trying to explain it—"it's the way you make a statement that you don't want to be kept alive . . . you know, artificially."

I felt my heart begin to race. "You mean—"

"Roger didn't want to live on and on in a coma, the way some people do. I wouldn't want that either, would you?"

"You mean . . . ," my voice cracked trying to get out the words. "Why don't you just say it? Roger doesn't want to live!"

I felt the pressure of her hands as she said, "He doesn't want to live *this* way. He wanted to have some control over his dying. Why should he suffer on and on just to please you and me?"

I hardly listened because my eyes kept filling and I kept blinking.

"So . . . so . . . what's so *living* about it?" I was practically shouting when I said, "I'd call that a dying will!"

Natalie let go of me, but she never looked away. " 'No heroic measures shall be taken.' That's what a living will says."

"Heroic!" I thought of my dad. "What's heroic about that? It's a cop-out if you ask me." I pulled away and stood up.

"I just wanted you to know, Buddy, in case they stop the IV and the oxygen. It's up to his daughter now. I thought"—Natalie's mouth turned down—"I just thought Roger's best friend should know."

She picked up Gary's coffee cup, set it on the tray by the microwave and walked out.

I left, too, and went on into the big supply room where the air was better, where our B & W can sat there on the hot pipes like some stupid pastime you don't care about anymore.

I leaned against the concrete wall. So they all knew. Mom probably knew, too. Roger was really going to die and they weren't going to save him this time, even if a little more oxygen would do the trick.

"Spring," Roger had said, "—tuliptime. We can be finished with that clipper ship by spring." He'd said that himself. Wasn't that something to live for?

And what about me? Don't I count? Can't you hang around a little longer for me? I've been hanging around you for two whole years!

I got up on the chair and pulled the can out of its place with my bare hand. I found the ballpoint, ripped out the paper, spread it there on the shelf. I didn't even look to see which list I was adding to.

"Die, then, if you want to so much!" I scrawled across the bottom in big writing.

Immediately I was ashamed. As ashamed as if Roger were there watching me, and I was so mad the paper shook in my hand. I didn't want to listen, but I could hear his voice saying, "It's what I want, Buddy." I hadn't wanted to listen the first time he'd said it, either.

I tore the paper into a million pieces, then stuffed the scraps back in the can and threw it onto the heat pipes.

There are no "Bests and Worsts" anymore, Natalie, just Worsts!

I went back upstairs and headed for Lucky Lucy's room, wishing I'd delivered her activity schedule when I did the others. There was no way I could tell her about Roger now without bawling my eyes out.

When I saw Lucy, her face told me she already knew. Agnes was lying on the far bed staring off, but Lucy was sitting there in her wheelchair as if she'd been waiting for me all day. She reached out and we hugged each other.

"Oh my, but you've been on my mind," she said. "Poor boy."

Quickly I turned around to change calendars on the

back of her door, swallowing and trying to get some control. I wondered who told her. I wondered if everyone in the nursing home knew Roger was dying.

"Have any lucky happenings today?" I said in a hard, cheery voice.

She wasn't listening. "Come sit here," she said when I finished.

I dropped down on the pink-and-white blanket on her bed and she wheeled as close to me as she could get.

Her eyes worked hard trying to focus on my face. "The unluckiest thing," she said, "is losing someone you love."

I nodded.

"All us old folks, we know that. But listen"—she pulled at my sleeve—"there's something else I learned—" The rest came out in whispers, but I heard every word: "You—never—really—lose 'em."

I studied her face and her eyes, which had grown bright with the effort of telling.

"You may think you lose 'em . . . ," she said, looking wise, "but you don't. Once you've loved somebody, they're part of your life."

I thought about her words long after I left the room. I thought about Roger and how he was already part of my life. I thought about my own father and how he'd been right there, in a way, in Thurston's office, reminding me of who I was.

I decided that Lucky Lucy, who couldn't beat her way out of a paper bag, had told me an important truth.

When I tiptoed in to say, "Goodnight, sleep tight," to Roger, the way my mom does with me, I felt a whole lot better.

CHAPTER ·18·

I went to school as usual the next day. On the way, Carmela and I talked about Roger and how sick he was. I told her about Mrs. Marti coming to be with him, and Carmela said she was glad. I also wanted her to know about Mr. Thurston playing football against my dad, but I couldn't find a way to bring it up.

Then she told me Mrs. Purdy had phoned her mom. "I'm now an official volunteer, like you. I'm going to bake Roger some cookies as soon as he starts feeling better." She glanced shyly my way. "You know, if you ever wanted me to, I could help you with that *shark* you're building."

I laughed, deciding Carmela was as big a tease as Roger. "You kidding? You've never built a model in your life! The *Cutty Sark* is advanced. It's not for beginners."

"I know a thing or two about following instructions," she said with a sniff. "I made a new skirt for Christmas and eight of the bibs we took to Sunnyside, including the fancy ones with the toggle-locks. Those were my own invention."

I acted like I was impressed. (I was!)

"Mama says I have a knack. Sometimes I'm better than she is at figuring out sewing patterns."

We said goodbye at Carmela's locker and the day settled into its normal gloomy pattern of wait and worry. I'd finally stopped praying. If what Natalie said was true—that it's cruel to keep someone suffering just to please yourself—then I wouldn't pray to keep Roger alive anymore.

It wasn't easy to come around to a new way of thinking. "A man develops strength where he needs it," Roger had said about his hands. I wondered if the same was true about a person's heart or his head. Roger and I were alike in lots of ways. We were both proud, both stubborn. Why couldn't I let him have his way when it came to something as big as death?

It was during sixth period when a kid delivered a note to my classroom from the office. It was for me. Mom must have phoned the school because it wasn't in her handwriting. All it said was, "Please come straight home today."

My hands grew cold after I read it. My whole body grew cold, even though my desk was only two feet from the hot air register.

I looked at the clock on the wall and wondered how it could have happened without some message from Roger. When the print in my social studies book started swimming in front of my eyes, I closed the book and put my head down on my arms.

For once I didn't run out of the building after school. I saw Carmela and Kim, but I didn't speak. I heard Jim Needham calling me, but I didn't turn around. I walked out of school in a trance, oblivious to the noise and the bodies brushing past.

I took my time getting home. A block away I could see Mom's car in the driveway. She never left Sunnyside until dinner was ready to be served, but today she was home. I knew why.

I opened the door and walked across the living room, into the dining room. Mom met me coming out of the kitchen and wrapped me in her arms. We stood there shaking for a long time before we could stop.

"He died early this morning," she said, wiping her eyes.

I pulled the sleeve of my parka across my face. "While I was asleep?"

"While we were all asleep."

"His daughter said it was very peaceful. He just"— Mom had a hard time saying it—"slipped away. They didn't have to face the hard decisions about taking him off the life-support systems—he died first. Isn't that typical of Roger? To be so considerate?"

I moved away and blinked hard at the window. I could see a ship slip into the water on its launching, something Roger had described to me in great detail. "It's beautiful," he'd said many times. "There are flags flying, bands playing . . . then in she goes, pretty as you please. There's a little spash as the displaced water comes back, slaps her sides, returns again. She's one with the ocean then."

I continued staring out the window. "Is that what she said—'slipped away'?"

I felt Mom's hands on my shoulders, the squeeze meaning "Yes" and "I'm sorry."

I went back to the living room, where I dropped into Mom's big chair without taking off my parka.

"Do you want anything?" she called from the kitchen.

"No."

A minute later she came into the living room carrying big old Myrtle. In spite of feeling terrible, seeing that pampered fern made me smile. I'd been so worried about Roger, I hadn't given Myrtle a thought.

"Smitty brought this huge thing over just before you got here. Said you were the one to have it. 'If Buddy does half as well with Roger's fern as he did taking care of Roger, it'll thrive.' That's what she said."

Mom looked around our cluttered living room. "Where on earth are we going to put another plant?"

I took Myrtle out of her hands; I also took back all the mean thoughts I ever sent Smitty's way.

"I have to go back, Tom, but I just couldn't stand having you walk in there . . ."

I nodded.

"You don't want to stay here by yourself, do you?"

I didn't answer right away because I was busy moving a pile of magazines so the fern could sit on the coffee table. "This won't be your permanent spot," I told Myrtle. "You'll want a north exposure."

I went to the nursing home in the car with Mom. Sooner or later, I knew, I had to face that empty nameplate and Roger's empty room.

She told me on the way that Roger's son would scatter his ashes somewhere in the North Atlantic. That's what he wanted, but right then the ocean seemed very far away. Maybe I'd plant a Bristlecone pine in back of the house where I could sit in the glider and watch it grow.

Mom parked in her usual spot and we went on in the kitchen entrance together. I hoped Mrs. Marti wouldn't be there, or even Natalie. I didn't want to see anyone else. Maybe I'd just go to the hold and stay there the whole time. Roger would want me to finish the *Cutty Sark*.

"Come on," Mom said after she hung her coat and put on her apron. "I'll go to his room with you. I've got time for that."

"It's okay, Mom, you don't have to—" But she did anyway.

We held hands walking along the hall, the way we did when I was four, and I didn't care who saw us. Roger was her friend, too. It had already occurred to me that *she* might be the one who couldn't stand to see room eighteen by herself.

I tried to keep my eyes off the nameplate as we neared his room, but I looked anyway and my heart leaped to see it wasn't empty yet.

"Look," I said, "his name—"

Mom made a little "oh" sound and we dropped hands.

I tried pretending everything was the same, that Roger would be there waiting for a trip to the greenhouse, but it only worked until we walked inside.

The housekeeper had already stripped the bed and angled it up for airing. The floor was shiny with new wax. Joe Hickson, the maintenance man, was down on his knees taking bolts out of the ship's wheel mounting.

"It's got to be crated and sent to Phoenix," he said when Mom asked.

I noticed the trawler lantern was gone, so I figured Mrs. Marti took that with her. I sighed looking around: a bed, a dresser, two chairs, a hospital table. It was an ordinary room with sunlight coming through the window.

I edged toward the door. "Will you be all right, Tom?" Mom asked.

"Yeah." I bumped against the trash can the house-keeper left sticking out, shoved it aside with my foot.

"Shall we go to McDonald's for hamburgers tonight?"

I heard Mom's voice, but my mind had swung around to what I just saw in the wastebasket: Roger's pipe . . . and the string of his tobacco pouch.

"McDonald's or a movie?" She asked again, trying to make me feel better.

"Can't we just have hamburgers at home?" I said when we got to the door of the hold.

"Of course we can." She left me then and went on to the kitchen to see to everyone's dinner.

Joe Hickson didn't notice a minute later when I reached down and took Roger's things from the wastebasket. I stuck the pipe and the soft black pouch in my coat pocket and headed for the exit.

I'd changed my mind about staying at Sunnyside. Suddenly I wanted to see Carmela. I know you don't usually have company while you're baby-sitting, but today was different. I wanted to ask if she meant it when she said she'd help me build the "shark" . . . and . . . I had to tell her about Roger.

I left the nursing home on a dead run and didn't stop until I got to where our street intersected Seventeenth.

Gulping in the air, I made myself slow to a walk so I could think about what I was going to say. I wanted to tell

Carmela how neat it was that Roger came along in my life at the exact precise time I needed him most. Maybe *I* came along at the right time for him, too.

The idea that came crowding in next gave me chills that had nothing to do with the cold. Roger had given me a present he didn't know anything about—a connection to my father that I didn't have before, even though I was his son. I couldn't tell Carmela *that!* I didn't understand it myself. But it had something to do with how much Roger and I liked and depended on each other.

There was something else on my mind, but I planned to call Troy and tell him about it first. I was going to sign up for track. "Since everybody wants me to so bad," I'd say on the phone, joking about the decision that had gnawed a hole clean through my stomach.

A cold wind funneled down our street, forcing my hands into the pockets of my parka where I found Roger's pipe. I stopped. I pulled it out, ran my fingers over the smooth stem and the rough-textured bowl. I held it to my nose and sniffed its tobacco smell. When I knocked it against my knee and nothing came out, I put it back in my pocket.

I started up again, thinking I probably should be crying or something, but the feelings I had right then were more peaceful than sad. Captain Ericksen was my great friend. I was his. I wouldn't be seeing him any more, but as Lucy said, he was part of me now. Remembering him wouldn't have to end—ever—unless I wanted it to.

I ducked my head into the wind and picked up my speed. The pipe nestled in my palm warmed me every step of the way to Carmela's house.